# NASHVILLE
## *by Heart*

a novel

## TINA ANN FORKNER

Published by Spavinaw Junction Press

This is a work of fiction. Names, characters, businesses, places, events and incidents are either the products of the author's imagination or used in a fictitious manner. Any resemblance to actual persons, living or dead, or actual events is purely coincidental.

ISBN-13: 979-8616237422

Author photo by Cheri Kaufman

*For my sister, Cheri Kaufman, and all who have followed their dreams to Nashville*

# Chapter One

From the moment Gillian boarded the bus for Nashville, she was a cliché, but she was about to change all that. Today, she refused to be just another small town girl with a guitar slung across her back. If that meant altering her style a little, then so be it. It wasn't like she was altering herself, right? Today, she was going to knock music manager Will Adams' boots off—even though, ironically, she wished she'd kept her boots on, instead of these crazy high heels she'd paid for with her last paycheck.

"Ms. Heart?"

She wobbled around to face the receptionist, her confidence whirling right out of her chest. If she'd been able to do more than stumble across the room in her heels, she might have galloped right out of there.

"That's me," she said, offering a smile as shaky as her balance. "Gillian."

The receptionist didn't respond immediately. She was too busy appraising Gillian's five-inch heels, shimmery silver top and the length of her skirt. Warmth flooded Gillian's face, but she balanced herself with a hand on one of the lobby's plush couches and forced herself to walk, albeit precariously, toward the reception desk. She didn't even want to know what the lady was thinking as she waited for Gillian to wobble her way across the room. By the time she got there, she felt like a ten-year-old in her momma's Sunday shoes. She attempted another smile, but when the lady frowned like one of those street mimes with painted-on emotions, Gillian couldn't keep the act up any more. Slouching, she frowned too.

"I'm Josie, Will's assistant." She stuck out her hand for Gillian to shake.

"Gillian," she repeated, shaking Josie's hand.

"I'm so sorry, sweetie." Josie's accent was even thicker than Gillian's. "Mr. Adams can't see you."

"What?" Gillian's voice croaked as she self-consciously tugged at her skirt. She couldn't help but squirm under the scrutiny of the receptionist's gaze. "Why?"

"He's having lunch with Audrey Smith, sweetie. Do you know who she is?"

"I've heard of her." Who hadn't heard of Audrey Smith, the newest and hottest star in country music?

"Audrey's his new client, but she's already got—"

"Three hit songs."

Josie smiled. "It sounds like you know your country music."

With effort, Gillian stood up straighter.

"Well," she said, trying to sound jovial. "We did have radios in Gold Creek Gap."

"Gold Creek Gap?" The assistant looked vaguely interested, or perhaps she was just pretending to be.

"Where I grew up."

"I see. Well, listen, Gillian." Josie walked toward the

door and motioned for her to follow. "I hope this doesn't sound all wrong, but while I'm not sure how you managed to get an appointment, I will let Mr. Adams know you came, honey. Does that help?"

"I talked to you on the phone," Gillian mumbled, trying to remember their conversation the week before. But now she wondered: Had she misunderstood?

"I don't recall that," Josie said, smiling brightly. "I'm sorry."

"Could we possibly reschedule?"

Josie blinked. "I'm so sorry. There's been a mistake. Mr. Adams does have an unplanned appointment that came up today, but honey, he only sees people who are experienced in the industry. He doesn't take on unknown talent."

Ouch. Josie wasn't smiling any more, and her pitying glance cut through Gillian. To hide the gathering tears, she stared down at her ridiculous shoes and felt her dreams evaporate. She heard Josie punch a button on the elevator door and waited for it to slide open. She couldn't look at the woman who'd so easily seen right through her confident veneer to the naïve dreamer she really was.

"I believe it's best to be honest," Josie said quietly, while they waited. "So can I give you some advice, honey?" She stuck out a hand to hold the elevator doors open.

"Please."

Catching her off guard, Josie lay a soft hand on her arm. The small act of kindness surprised Gillian, making her long suddenly for Gold Creek Gap, where everyone loved her and she never had to pretend. It took effort to look at Josie.

"I can tell you're very pretty," Josie said. "Underneath all that makeup."

Gillian placed a hand on the wall for balance, but ended up grasping Josie's outstretched hand instead.

Josie let the elevator door close.

"Why don't you take those silly shoes off, honey? You obviously don't know how to walk in them."

Gillian ignored the heat in her cheeks and kicked off the heels. Any pretense she was holding onto left in a puff of air from her lips as she groaned in pleasure at the sweet release of setting her toes free.

"I feel like such a phony," she said. "Please know, this isn't me, I just thought—"

"You wouldn't be the first," Josie said. "Girls like you are always trying to doll themselves up and be someone they're not, but with you, I can see right through it."

"Is that a compliment?" Gillian flashed a half-hearted smile.

"Sure is. Wipe off half that makeup and try wearing a pair of boots to your next audition."

Gillian touched her cheek, absently rubbing the makeup away already. She felt ridiculous, and at twenty-five years old, it seemed like Josie, who must have only been a few years her elder, was decades ahead when it came to business know-how.

"And if you play an instrument, bring it," Josie said. "This *is* Nashville."

"Got it," Gillian said, wishing she'd brought her momma's guitar. She watched Josie push the button again. The doors slid open, and if she could've crawled into the elevator and died, she might've been better off, but something about Josie's kind tone froze her in place. She took a deep breath. She didn't want to leave on a bad note, just in case she was ever invited back. Although she was pretty sure that'd never happen.

"Anything else?" Gillian tried not to look desperate.

"Don't give up, honey. Maybe try back in a few months, when you have some more experience under your belt."

"Gotcha." She felt like her three years in Nashville counted for something, but of course, there she was being turned away again. Maybe she was wrong. "Thanks for the advice."

Josie offered a small smile and waved goodbye. As soon as the elevator doors closed, Gillian's hands flew to her face. She kept it together until the elevator stopped and the doors slid open. Not bothering to look around, she hurried through the lobby, shoes in hand, and ducked into the ladies' room. That's when she wilted.

"Don't cry, don't cry, don't cry." But she did.

Staring wide-eyed into the mirror, she dropped the shoes and fanned her already wet lashes with both hands. Why had she dressed like this? She'd given Josie the impression she was as fake as her new eyelashes. Gillian couldn't blame the sweet receptionist, but the realization that she had looked ridiculous made her feel like an even bigger fool. Ducking into a stall, she plopped down on the toilet lid and buried her face in her hands.

Momma would be disappointed.

What'd she been thinking? That she looked good dressed that way? And that Will Adams, one of the busiest music managers in the industry, would actually give her the time of day?

But yes, as outrageous as it was, that's exactly what she'd thought. She still remembered when the receptionist, it must have been Josie, actually returned her call. Gillian had spilled her iced tea all over herself trying to get a pen to write down the appointment. After that, she'd stressed for days, spending way too much time picking out her clothes. She'd practiced her best songs over and over, ready to impress Will Adams, but apparently it was all a fluke. And she'd forgotten her guitar.

Now, she'd have to go to her shift at the café where her friends, almost all struggling musicians and singers themselves, waited to hear how it went. She'd have to tell them she was a big fat failure. Again.

"No, not a failure," she whispered in an effort to recover her pride, thinking of what her momma would say. *This is just a setback.*

Oh, how she wanted to call her momma right then, but she resisted. One day, she'd call home with a big announcement, like a record deal, but never with news that she was a fake and a failure.

Desperately wiping at her lipstick with a wad of toilet paper, she stifled a sob. She'd stupidly bought the kind that stayed on for hours. That was an extra thirty dollars she couldn't get back. In fact, the mere thought of all the money she'd wasted on what was supposed to be a sexy, sophisticated country look made her feel like she'd just lost everything in Vegas. She glanced down at her bare legs sticking out from what she now realized was an incredibly short skirt. Wearing it had seemed like such a good idea at the time.

"Gee Manetti, I look like a Vegas showgirl."

She was glad no one was in the bathroom to hear her arguments with herself. On someone else, the skirt might have been perfect, but not on her. She looked like a little girl playing dress-up. With a deep sigh, she stared at her ridiculous reflection for a few more seconds, then straightened to her full height. Her height was one thing she'd always had going for her. Josie was right. She didn't need those heels.

"The show must go on."

She smoothed her hair, tugged her skirt down—not that it helped any—slipped her feet back into her shoes, because they were all she had, and exited the bathroom in a hurry.

"Howdy."

Now self-conscious of her outfit, she ducked her head and barely glanced at the man standing beside the door. Hopefully she could get past him and out of the building with just a mumbled hello.

"It's raining," he announced. "Reckon we should wait it out?"

She glimpsed the glass doors, and sure enough, sheets of rain showered the sidewalk outside. The drops pelted the glass, filling the lobby with a low roar. She must have been too upset to hear it in the bathroom.

"Good gravy." She shook her head in frustration and stomped her foot, which was a bad idea that made her start to wobble again. Regaining her balance, she planted her fists on her hips. Of course. Of course, this would be her day. It'd barely been overcast when she'd taken the bus to Music Row that morning, so she hadn't bothered with an umbrella.

"Are you lost?"

Now, why would he think she was lost?

"No. I'm fine, thanks."

"Have a nice day then."

She glanced at him. Heavens, he was handsome.

She stopped, wobbled again, and accidentally smiled just a little. Very handsome. And he definitely wasn't the doorman in those jeans. She frowned, unwilling to interact with a stranger—even this one—at this very complicated and frustrating moment.

"Forget something?" he asked.

Caught off guard, she shook her head and turned toward the safety of the ladies' room. Then she tripped. Gasping, she tried to catch herself, but instead a pair of strong hands grasped her waist, jerking her upright.

"Whoa." He gripped her arm with one strong hand while reaching down to retrieve her dropped purse. She glanced quickly at his ring finger. Single. Her eyes locked with his.

Holy cow. Who in the world has eyes so blue? They drew her into a mesmerizing tide of crystal clear allure.

He smiled, and after what she'd just endured, it would have been nice to be swept away by a handsome stranger, but that would be ridiculous. Finally realizing she was staring, she tore her eyes away and stared down at his boots.

"You OK?" he asked.

Catching a whiff of some kind of leathery scent that reminded her of her dad, she dared another peek. He was smiling with a self-assured expression that might have come across as cocky if not for the way he looked at her, like she was the only one who mattered in that instant. That was like her dad too, which wasn't necessarily a good thing, but she couldn't seem to make herself say goodbye and walk away.

"I'm fine," she said, still teetering around like a puppet on a string.

He held the purse out. "You'd better take this. It's not really my style."

She nearly dropped it again. "Thanks."

Great. As if the morning could get any worse. Now she was making a fool of herself in front of a man who was too attractive to be real, except that she could still feel his hand grasping her arm. If only she could again take off the stilt shoes that were throwing her off balance, but that would be awkward—plus, she needed them on to get home.

"Gotcha," he said, gently tightening his grip when she stumbled again. When he lightly took her other arm in his, she found herself locked in his gaze. She stood there, knowing she should leave before she did something nonsensical, like cry or laugh out loud. She wasn't sure which one the situation warranted. He smiled again, flashing almost perfect teeth, except one slightly crooked eye tooth that you wouldn't even notice unless you were this close to him. She took a breath, admitting to herself that she kind of liked the position she found herself in, even though the circumstances of how she got there weren't all that desirable, and he was a total stranger.

She took another good look at him. A stranger who was familiar.

Maybe it was his confident air, or maybe he was a famous country singer. Who knew in Nashville? He even had a scruffy Keith Urban quality that kept throwing her off.

"Steady, there." His low drawl resounded in her ears in a pure Tennessee accent. Well, he wasn't Australian, so definitely not Keith Urban. Her world rocked sideways even though he held her steady. She felt anything but as he stared at her with that crooked smile.

She noted his glance down, eyes quickly taking in her outfit from the wobbly shoes, grazing up her long legs and silky blouse before resting on her stained-red mouth, and, finally, her misty eyes. She looked away, wishing she could dash back into the safety of the bathroom, but he still held her. It was a good thing, too, with how off-kilter she was at the moment.

She really wished she'd worn her boots. One thing was for sure, Cinderella was wrong about the impression a fancy pair of shoes can make. She was now swaying like a bad line dancer.

"I've got you." He definitely did. Gathering her dignity, she hoped he couldn't see how he made blood rush to her head.

"You need to sit down or something, darlin'?"

So, he was one of those guys. The kind who called women darlin', as if there was already some kind of connection between them. She hated the type, at least usually. There didn't seem to be anything especially creepy about this guy though. His voice echoed concern.

She opened her mouth, and for the first time since she'd come to Nashville, she was speechless. *Really? Now?*

Since thinking of something to say was impossible, she snapped it shut before she resembled Loretta, her pet goldfish.

"No… thanks. I'm OK," she finally said, regaining her balance. He cautiously let go, then offered his hand to shake.

"Will Adams. And you are?"

She blinked. *The* Will Adams she'd come here to meet? Her heart drummed, and she could've sworn she heard a clang in her ears. Will Adams. Get yourself together, girl, she told herself, and she did.

"Gillian." She stuck out her hand as calmly as she could, thinking maybe her luck was turning around—or getting worse. At this point it was hard to tell. He responded by wrapping his fingers around hers. They were warm, and he didn't immediately let go, which gave her time to study his face. His relative success in the music business, and pictures she'd seen of him, had led her to assume he was at least in his forties. Up close, she could see he was only five or six years her senior, maybe around thirty or so.

"Do you have a last name, Gillian?" His gaze locked on hers.

"Heart."

He squinted, apparently pondering her name. His fingers, still wrapped gently around hers, made her forget for a split second why she was there.

"Gillian Heart," he said. "Nice to meet you. Are you lost?"

"Lost?" Yes, but no. She shook her head. She wasn't lost, even though he obviously didn't remember cancelling their appointment not fifteen minutes ago.

Maybe she *had* misunderstood.

"I had an appointment with you," she muttered. "Or at least I thought I did." She stared at their hands, his grip gentle, but still securely holding hers in place.

He smiled, his blue eyes drawing her in like magic. She thought she might swoon with all the butterflies flitting around inside her chest, so she reached for a nearby countertop. He let her go. She closed her fingers into a fist, trapping the warmth inside.

"*You* had an appointment with *me*?"

"I thought so."

"Hmm. I don't recall havin' you on my schedule," he drawled. He didn't mention rescheduling. "Unfortunately I gotta run though. I'm havin' lunch with—" He aimed a thumb toward the door, and Gillian suspected a brush off. She could see it now. He'd been interested in her, but as soon as he found out she was trying to get signed by him, he was finished.

"Audrey," she said, inching toward the door. He inched after her. "Josie told me."

He smiled again, making her knees turn to jelly. Trying not to wobble, she looked for a new place to rest her hand. The exit wasn't close enough to grip, so he held his arm out like a dashing prince. This was very much like a fairytale, but it didn't seem to be headed toward a happy ending at all.

"Right. Lunch with Audrey," he said, staring at her hand for a minute, seeming to be pondering her presence in his lobby. "But hey, Gillian. You sing, right?"

"That's why I'm here," she said with what she knew was a goofy smile. She was definitely not in flirting mode. She reluctantly let go of his arm and took her chances, knowing it was pointless to hope he would be either a manager or a date now. Warmth filled her cheeks yet again. She was having quite the embarrassing day.

"Thanks," she said. "I'll let you get to your meeting now."

"Why don't you get some music to me?" he called after her. "I'll give it a listen, as an apology for cancelling our meeting."

She stopped short. "Really?"

Holy cow. What should she do? She patted her tiny skirt pockets, as if the answer could be in there, then remembered her purse.

"Oh, then in that case I have something now."

She dug through her purse like a mad woman, her heart pounding, until she produced a CD with her name written on the case in red permanent marker.

He chuckled. "Old school, are we?"

Her face, already flushed, was now like a flame lighting a watchtower. Stupid, stupid, stupid. Of course, probably nobody used CDs any more. They'd email a digital file or something. Maybe hand him a thumb drive. Send him to a website, which she didn't have. She'd listed herself on some aspiring artist sites but couldn't even remember which ones they were. She took back the CD. No wonder she didn't have a record deal yet. Heck, do they still call them record deals?

"I'm sorry." She attempted to stuff the CD back in her purse. "I recorded it at home… uh… back in… my hometown, you know, we didn't have a… never mind. I guess it is old school."

"You don't say." His eyes softened. "I like old school."

She wondered if he saw through the makeup to the scared little girl behind it. She hoped not.

"I like it a lot," he said, indicating for her to give the CD back to him. "I'll let you know what I think. We can talk about it over lunch some time, if you want."

Her heart raced, and she couldn't think of a single word, even though all she needed to say was yes. After being humiliated by her encounter with his assistant, this was the last possible thing she'd expected to happen. And forget about those tiny little leaps her heart had been making when he looked at her; she was now weak in the knees from more than attraction. He wanted to meet with her about music, after all. How lucky could she get? And after making so many amateur mistakes in one day.

"What do you say?" he was asking. "I know a great sushi place."

Her nose wrinkled involuntarily. What kind of Southerner was he?

She thought about joking with him that anyone who'd eat raw fish was crazy, but she didn't want to offend him, especially if he was going to listen to her music.

"Does that sound good?" he asked.

It sounded awful. Maybe she was just a bundle of nerves, but the very thought of raw fish made her stomach turn. In her world, fish were meant to be battered and fried.

"Maybe," she said, giving him a smile that felt as wobbly as her feet in those ridiculous shoes.

*Please,* she thought—*anything but sushi.*

# Chapter Two

Holy smokes. Will was having a hard time tearing his eyes away from the girl standing—no, wobbling—in his building's lobby and telling him that *maybe* they could have sushi together. Everything about her appearance was incredibly distracting, including her green eyes sparkling even brighter than her glittery eyeshadow and all that blond hair hanging like silk across her shoulders. He didn't know where to look that didn't send his mind into a swirl of thoughts that had nothing to do with music. Tearing his gaze away from her mouth, he focused on what she'd said.

*Maybe.*

He grinned. "Maybe you'll have lunch with me? Or maybe you'll have sushi?"

She opened her mouth to say something but immediately snapped it shut.

"Don't tell me," he said. "Sushi not your thing?"

The way she wobbled in those crazy shoes convinced him she wasn't accustomed to wearing them—or eating sushi.

"Sushi's definitely not my thing," she said in a quiet voice. He couldn't help but smile. She made him think of his sisters who still lived where they all grew up in a small town outside of Gatlinburg. Sushi wasn't their thing either—too citified, they always said—although every time they visited, he begged them to try it.

"Forget the sushi," he said.

"But—" She looked panicked, and her voice hit an odd high note. "I'd still like to see, er, meet with you."

She was clearly nervous. Wannabe clients always were, and he didn't blame them. In his mind, he was still Will, a country boy from a big family, but to aspiring musicians, he was a genie who could grant their wishes if they didn't rub him the wrong way. He didn't think Gillian could rub him the wrong way at all.

Of course, he hadn't heard her sing, but he'd like to.

"It's a date," he said.

He hadn't realized how the word "date" might sound until he'd already said it and she'd turned an enchanting shade of pink. To be honest, if it turned out she couldn't sing a lick, he'd happily take her out on a real date, but only if she traded in those crazy-looking heels for some regular shoes, preferably a pair of boots. But she could keep that skirt.

"OK," she said, standing a little straighter despite her obvious discomfort.

He wished he could put her at ease. The playing field was not level at all, but he sure would like to toss off his agent hat and get down on her level. As soon as he thought it, he mentally slapped himself for being such a rake. There was a time when he wouldn't have had any problem mixing business with pleasure, but he was a gentleman now.

"What about fried catfish?" he asked. "Chicken?"

She laughed, the sudden lilt in her voice making him

grin wider. He listed a half dozen Southern foods, all fried.

"And we can talk about your music," he added.

"I guess I like anything, if we're talking about music," she said.

Her shy smile gave him a glimpse of a woman more down-to-earth than her makeup and outfit suggested. He wanted to know that person.

"Anything except sushi," he said, grinning.

"Except for sushi."

"Then it's settled."

She nodded agreement but said nothing as she fiddled with the fringe on her purse.

He knew he should say goodbye and get going—Audrey would be ticked at him for being late—but instead he stood rocking on his heels like a school boy about to ask a girl to the dance. He could definitely imagine taking her out on the dance floor, rocking the night away, but first they'd have to do something about those shoes. Not that he completely hated them on her. They were sexy. She just couldn't stand up in the damn things.

"It's settled," she said, the pink filling her cheeks again. He'd like to think it was all because of him, but he knew better. A chance to share her music with him would feel like a once-in-a-lifetime opportunity. Even though there was something about Gillian Heart that made him want to know more on a personal level, he had to admit there was some star quality about her, too, and it wasn't only because she was gorgeous. Call it his agent's sixth sense, but he knew better than to ignore that feeling.

He smiled, hoping to put her at ease. "You haven't been in Nashville long, have you?"

"About three years." She took a deep breath, perhaps to calm her nerves, but she looked about as calm as a pressure cooker, and to be honest, about as hot too. And there he went again, needing to mentally slap himself.

Trying to be a gentleman, he kept his eyes focused on her face. He was used to his presence making potential clients nervous, but he wasn't accustomed to them making his mind spin out of control.

"In Nashville time, you practically just got here," he said.

She offered a smile, and he thought it could light up a whole crowd. "I guess so. Sometimes it feels like forever."

He nodded, understanding how she felt. He'd seen a lot of girls in her shoes. Well, maybe not *those* shoes, he mused, but she might not realize how common it was to be in Nashville for years and not have a record deal. He knew a slew of musicians who'd been performing in Nashville for twenty and still didn't have a deal.

"Well, don't ever give up," he said, despite the fact that statistics told him she would. He hoped she wasn't one of them and was pleased to see a flash of hope in her eyes. There was a time when he had that same look in his own eyes, before he got into music management.

"Thanks," she said, and her smile reminded him of someone he knew. He knew a songwriter by the same last name. Maybe they were related, but before he could ask, she glanced toward the doors, obviously ready to leave.

"Looks like the rain's quit." He thought a look of relief crossed her face.

"Before we go, what's the plan?" he asked. "We don't even have to eat. We can meet back here in my office later. Or how about a drink? I know a little bar around the corner…"

He'd been thinking a drink was more informal and less intimidating than lunch or a meeting in his office, at least that's what he told himself, but her nervous look was back. She was ready to bolt, and he wasn't ready to let her.

"I have to work." She gave him an apologetic look. "I'm a waitress."

"Of course you are," he said, smiling. They were always waitresses. "Just give Josie a call. She schedules everything."

"I will."

He waved the CD. "And I'll listen."

She nodded, but he couldn't tell if it was a yes or another maybe. Taking her hand in a goodbye shake, he realized she was trembling. Giving her what he hoped was a calming smile, he let her go, noticing her smooth pale nails as her hand slipped from his. They were completely void of polish, which didn't match the tone of anything else she was wearing. He smiled to himself, pretty sure that if she were to wipe off all that makeup, a natural born country girl would emerge. That's what he liked to see in a client, but rarely found any more. So much of country music was all about being flashy these days.

"Thanks a bunch," she said. "I'll see you later."

His heart raced at the thought of seeing her again, but unlike her, his experience as an agent had taught him how to hide his emotions. He glanced at his watch—a vintage gift from his parents—remembering he had to get going too, but couldn't help stealing another minute. His music agent side wondered how she'd look on stage as he surreptitiously glanced at the string of beads draped across her chest, the only thing at all country about her outfit, then the man side of him glanced down a little lower before raising his gaze to meet her eyes.

Caught staring, he cleared his throat and looked at his boots. He was a jerk, but that skirt and those silly high heels sent his mind in directions they shouldn't go if he was thinking about giving her a chance as a client.

She smiled then, making him wonder if she knew the effect she was having on him. She had to.

"I know you've gotta get going," she said. "So do I."

But he didn't want her to go. In fact, he wanted to take her home right in broad daylight, but somehow he knew that underneath that sexy outfit, she wasn't the type. And then he wouldn't be able to pursue her as a client. It was a frustrating, and enticing, quandary he found himself in. Fortunately, even though he was having trouble curbing his roaming thoughts, he was a changed man. His former womanizing ways went all the way back to when his preacher dad kicked him out for trying to steal his girlfriend's virginity in the back of the church van—as well as for stealing the van and a long list of other things. As a thirty-year-old man, he'd redeemed himself to his father a long time ago, but sometimes, when he was around a beautiful woman like Gillian Heart, he turned back into a bit of a Casanova.

"Right, I do need to get out of here," he said, wishing it weren't true, but glad too. "I'll see you soon. Just call Josie."

She nodded, bobbing a little sideways.

He grinned, watching her rush toward the revolving door that spun her out of the Adams Music offices and away from Music Row.

From the window he could see her hurrying down the sidewalk, toward the bus stop he presumed. Holy smokes. The jut of her cute little chin and the maddening wiggle of her hips from walking in those terrible shoes was delightful—even if he did prefer cowgirl boots on a woman.

He hurried through the doors himself and stood staring after her. He was just in time to see her stop and remove her shoes. She looked back, giving him the tiniest wave before disappearing around the corner.

He cocked his head and smiled, glad he'd kept her

CD, if for no other reason than to have an excuse to see her again. He hoped he didn't have to break her heart about her voice, which would completely mess up any possibility of taking her out. Then again, if she could sing, that would mess everything up too.

కు

Will glanced at his buzzing phone. It was a text from Audrey. Her time was precious. Everybody's time in Nashville was precious, but since she was his most promising new star, he obeyed her summons. Climbing into his brand new black truck, he left to meet her at The Sweetest Tea Café, but he slowed his truck when he spotted Gillian at the bus stop around the corner, standing beautiful—and steady—without those blasted shoes of hers. He chuckled, watching her disappear in his rearview mirror, then pressed down on the gas pedal. He was already late.

On cue, his phone rang. "Yep, Audrey. I got your message. On my way."

Audrey was his ticket to get out of this mess the business had fallen into. And even though she was the newest big name in Nashville, she'd paid her dues by singing back-up for an impressive list of country music stars and performing at the best honky-tonk bars in Nashville. She was his sure thing when it came to clients. Even if some of her recent stardom had gone to her head, her years of experience in the industry made her a hell of a lot easier to work with than the boy and girl scouts who tried daily to get an appointment with him.

He flipped on the radio. Of course, Audrey never made blood gush to his head like Gillian Heart had. That reminded him of the CD he'd tossed onto the seat beside him. He popped it in just for kicks, and about thirty seconds in, slammed on the breaks, nearly causing an accident. He pulled into the closest parking lot and turned up the volume.

Holy smokes.

# Chapter Three

"What happened?" Tasha tied the straps of her Sweetest Tea Café apron and handed Gillian hers. "Did he come on to you? He used to have a reputation, you know. I would've been more than happy if he'd made a pass at me."

"No, not exactly." But then she thought about how he'd held her hand when he probably should've let go, not that she'd pulled away either, and the lingering way he'd looked at her.

"Well," she said. "For a minute I thought he might ask me out if I wasn't there looking for an agent."

"You drove him crazy in those sexy high heels, didn't you?"

Gillian laughed. Maybe that's all it was. She might be naïve about some things, having grown up in a small town, but she wasn't stupid. Will Adams had been attracted to her, but it probably was the shoes. And the length of her skirt. And maybe the shirt too. There's no way it could've simply been because of her mesmerizing personality. She'd realized too late that dressing in a way that made some girls look classy made her look like a tart. Obviously he'd been attracted.

"I made a fool of myself," Gillian said, doubting Will Adams would have a hard time pulling his eyes away once he saw her dressed like her normal, plain self—if he ever saw her again at all. Now that she was away from Music Row, the magical hope that had followed her on the bus trip back had evaporated into anxiety.

"A fool? How?"

Gillian pointed at her eyes. "Look at my face."

"Not a good color for you," Tasha said. "Just being honest."

"You could've told me that this morning when you said I looked fancy."

"Sorry, bad lighting in our apartment, but you did look fancy."

Gillian sighed. "So the big question is, does he want to talk about my singing? Or does he just want to see me in those high heels again?"

"Maybe both," Tasha said.

Gillian rolled her eyes.

"Listen, honey. Who cares? Right now you don't really have a horse in the race, do you?"

"You know I don't," Gillian said, her face softening.

"Then onward and upward. Be glad he noticed you at all."

Happy-go-lucky Tasha always knew how to put things in perspective. In the time Gillian had known her, she'd made a lot of the big worries seem small. They'd been roommates since Gillian answered an ad in the newspaper: ASPIRING FEMALE MUSIC ARTIST SEEKING LIKE-MINDED FEMALE ROOMMATE.

She wasn't sure how like-minded they were, besides both being aspiring singers, but Tasha's no-holds-barred city girl personality hadn't clashed with Gillian's small-town girl sensibilities as much as one might expect. She couldn't have asked for a better roommate. Plus, Tasha had gotten Gillian a job at The Sweetest Tea Café. She owed her the world for that alone.

Tasha plucked a pen from the checkout counter.

"So, then what?"

"So, then he asked me to meet him for sushi and to talk about music—and I said maybe."

"Who eats sushi?" Tasha shuddered in her slightly too-snug waitress uniform, making her curly brown ponytail swish. Apparently dislike of sushi was on their short list of like-minded ideas, which was a good thing. Neither one of them could afford sushi anyway.

"Wait a minute." Tasha arched her penciled-in brows. "You told him *maybe*?"

"I know. I'm an idiot."

"Well, that's an idiotic answer even if you don't like sushi, girl! Will Adams could make or break your career."

Gillian's heart dropped to the linoleum floor as the ridiculousness of it sank in. He didn't seem like the type to break someone's career, she thought, remembering how he'd gently steadied her in the lobby, but he was probably just being nice.

"I agreed to meet with him," she said. "But not for sushi."

"So you're going on a date?"

"To talk about music."

"Lucky you," Tasha said. "I'd go out with him even if he didn't want to talk about music. He *is* easy on the eyes, don't you think?" She waggled her eyebrows.

"Totally hot." Gillian, in fact, hadn't been able to stop thinking about him towering over her—even next to her height—with those strong shoulders and piercing, but kind, eyes. The ridiculous swirl of excitement in her chest hadn't gone away after leaving Adams Music, and it wasn't only about the chance to sign as a client with him either. He was sexy, intensely attractive, and wildly confident. In fact, he was exactly the kind of man her momma had warned her about. And after her last relationship, she wanted to avoid anyone likely to break her heart.

"He's hot," she reiterated. "But you know my rule."

"Oh sure." Tasha rolled her eyes. "No time for men until you've got a record deal, but at the rate music deals are being handed out, you might be deal-less *and* man-less forever if you don't at least use what your momma gave you."

Gillian knew Tasha meant well, but she'd used what her momma gave her to get noticed at her cancelled meeting today, and while Tasha might've been able to pull it off with her playful personality, it'd made her feel cheap when Josie looked her up and down.

"You aren't me," Gillian said, reaching for the coffee pot. "Your mom has been married for thirty years. You don't know how bad men can be. I'd probably be wise to avoid him any other way except as an agent."

"Well, your momma got to have you out of whatever happened in her relationship, so I don't see how it was all that bad."

Gillian sighed. She didn't know where her dad was right now. He might even be in Nashville, but he'd given her up completely when he'd left her mother and her own musical dreams in Gold Creek Gap. And then there was Robert, whom she'd met in Nashville her first year. He'd turned out to be just like her dad. Momma had been right about him too.

"Momma knows how Nashville is."

"Was," Tasha corrected. "No disrespect to your sweet momma, honey, but she was here trying to make it more than twenty-five years ago, right?"

"Some things don't change," Gillian said. "Like men." Last she'd heard, her ex was still making his rounds among the Nashville starlets, like her dad had done. And to think she'd entertained the idea of marrying Robert.

Tasha shook her head. "Oh yeah. Men are so evil, since the beginning of time. They might tempt you to do something wild, like fall in love, get married and…" She gasped, mockingly. "Heaven forbid—have a posse of kids and distract you from pursuing the elusive music contract."

"You make it sound like a crazy dream, but yeah, something like that." Gillian gave a little laugh.

Tasha shook her head. "Loretta Lynn didn't let all those kids stop her. Nobody says you have to fall in love, but it'd be OK to let a man take you out to a real dinner, especially a rich one like Will Adams—just maybe not for sushi."

"I'd even have sushi if it meant a free meal," commented another waitress as she breezed past them.

"I rest my case," Tasha said. "And don't worry if it's a date or business."

Gillian said nothing, but shuddered remembering the few dates she'd gone on when she first got to Nashville, before she met Robert. She'd been homesick and had no friends, so she'd let Tasha drag her out to the honky-tonks. The men she met had all been as dumb as fence posts and didn't even hide what they were after. When she wouldn't sleep with them, they said things like, "But I took you to dinner!" or "I bought you a beer!" And Gillian's favorite, "But I know the head of a record label. I can get you in. Just slide on over here, sweetheart." Ugh.

Patting her apron pockets, Gillian checked for the order pad and pen, even though she rarely used them, so accustomed was she to taking orders by heart. And it was her heart, as well as her goal of getting a record deal, that she needed to protect. She'd almost forgotten to keep her guard up. No matter how adorable Will Adams was, she'd do well to remember her plan. She'd learned while growing up in Gold Creek Gap that men tied you down to home, stole your dreams and then left. She vividly remembered how she'd begged her songwriter dad to take her along on his monthly drives to Nashville. Then one time, he'd hugged her a little bit longer than normal, and never came back.

"Maybe Will Adams wasn't serious about meeting at all," she said, wondering if she'd misunderstood again. "He is a man. He'll probably stand me up."

"He might," Tasha said. "But then again, what if he doesn't? May be your big break."

"I hope you're right," Gillian said. "Onward and hopefully upward, right?"

She moved toward her assigned table section to pour coffee while Tasha headed for the VIP room. Gillian would usually kill to serve all the important locals, but today she wanted to be around regular people.

The café's owner, June, paused beside her. "Hey, honey. I heard about the meeting."

"Already? No secrets in this place."

"No, there aren't, but if Will wants to talk to you again, that's huge." She smiled her trademark red lipstick grin. That was how to wear red lipstick, Gillian noted. Not the way she'd worn it earlier that day.

"I think he felt sorry for me," she said.

June dismissed the comment with a flick of her wrist. "Men like Will Adams don't have time for meetings because they feel sorry for you. You've got to believe in yourself."

"I'm trying," Gillian said.

"Well, keep trying," June said. "I've seen a lot of girls go home, and I've seen some make it too. I think you've got what it takes, sugar."

"Thanks." Gillian ducked to hide the blush of her

cheeks, truly touched that June believed in her. June was probably on the younger side of thirty, looked like a star herself and knew everything about Nashville, particularly the music industry. Everyone who was anyone came to her restaurant, and she treated them like royalty. She even gave the true country music royals their own room to dine in. She treated regular people the exact same way.

"Oh, while I'm thinking about it," June said. "We're gonna have a lot of leftovers tonight. You girls don't forget to dish up a bunch and take 'em home. I don't like throwing away food."

"That'd be great. Thank you." And Gillian meant it. After the money she'd spent on the bus fare and the new outfit she'd bought for her failed meeting with Will Adams, she didn't know if she had enough change left to stock her half of the fridge. Grateful, she hastened to get coffee for the customers.

She was so busy that the next half hour passed quickly. When the bell above the door jingled, she glanced up to see if anyone was available to help the waiting customers.

"Oh, shoot." There in the doorway was Will Adams and his next big thing, Audrey. Audrey was looking gorgeous, all curly blond hair, denim and boots. Gillian wanted to duck, but that would be silly, so she stood holding her coffee pot in one hand, frozen. Luckily, Will Adams' gaze passed right over her. She must not have been recognizable with her hair pulled back in a ponytail and wearing a blue fifties-style waitress dress.

When another waitress greeted the pair, Gillian breathed a sigh of relief. The morning had been crazy enough with the high heels and lipstick. The last thing she wanted for the next time he saw her was to be dressed like the 1950s. Next time she wanted to look like herself, but as she made a move to pour coffee for someone, she realized it was too late. She overfilled the coffee cup, causing a commotion of clattering dishes, spoons and apologies. She pulled a cloth from her apron and mopped up the mess, and when she glanced up, Will's eyes were resting on hers. He smiled.

Without thinking, she smiled back and ridiculously held the coffee pot up in a kind of salute. His smile widened, and for a second he looked like he might be about to head her way, but Audrey popped back through the curtain, laced her arm through his, and they were gone, the curtain swinging closed behind them.

"I'm so sorry," Gillian told the man whose coffee she spilled. "I'll give you more coffee."

Trying to forget that Will was seated in the very next room, Gillian paid special attention to her customers, even scrubbing a few of the tabletops for the overwhelmed busboys.

"Don't take the Formica off," Tasha said a few minutes later. "I need you to trade me places."

"Why?" But Gillian knew why.

"You need to be waiting on Will Adams," she hissed. "I heard him talking about you."

"Me?"

"Yes, you, Sherlock." Tasha rattled off Will's order. "Now go and tell him about tonight at The Blue Fiddle."

"Oh my gosh!" Gillian slapped the side of her head with the rag.

"Gross," Tasha said, snatching the rag away. "You know what that rag has wiped up?"

Gillian laughed, grabbing a clean towel and wiping at the side of her face.

"This day is so wild. I don't even know what I'm doing. My mind is racing."

"Well, I don't think Marv would like you forgetting about The Blue Fiddle," Tasha said. "You'd better readjust your brain. And go in the VIP room and get your man."

"My agent," Gillian corrected.

"Whatever. Just go get him."

Gillian smiled, still nervous, but empowered. She'd almost forgotten about her performance that night at The Blue Fiddle, where she waitressed nights with Tasha. She felt so blessed to be a regular opening act for her boss, Marv. Why hadn't she told Will Adams about it?

"What should I say?"

Tasha smiled. "I took his order, so go back to the kitchen, get it and say with a smile, here's your chicken fried steak."

"Like it'll be that easy. I'll probably spill his coffee like I did to that poor man earlier."

"It will be easy. Trust me."

Gillian headed toward the kitchen, rehearsing what she'd say under her breath.

"Hi. Here's your chicken fried steak. And would you like to watch me sing tonight?"

"I'd love to," a pimple-faced young man sitting at a table of men called out.

She paused and laughed at herself. She obviously hadn't been as quiet as she thought. The boy, who was a regular customer, grinned.

"Where are you singing, sweetheart?" He tried to look taller.

She adopted a motherly voice. "You have to be twenty-one to go, sweetheart."

His shoulders sagged, but he still smiled as his older friends guffawed and slapped his back.

"Well, good luck!" he called, blushing. "You'll be great."

"Why, thank you, honey." She walked back and filled his coffee cup a little bit more, hoping that he was right.

# Chapter Four

Seeing Gillian Heart at The Sweetest Tea Café froze Will in his tracks. She looked a lot different than when he'd met her that morning in the lobby of his office.

"Well, I'll be damned."

The waitress outfit was cute, but heck, he would've felt the same jolt of attraction no matter what she had on. And that voice he'd heard on the CD. It was a lot bigger than one would expect from someone like her, and it excited him as much as her looks. He was already picturing her as a fresh-faced, small town girl with a guitar—*more denim and pearls than leather and lace,* he thought.

"Who's she?" Audrey wanted to know.

Will tore his eyes away. "That's Gillian Heart."

He gave Audrey the short version of their cancelled meeting as they slid into their booth.

"It's not like you to see amateurs," she said, clicking her pink manicured nails on the Formica tabletop.

He studied Audrey. It wasn't like her to be threatened

by a potential client.

"I felt bad about cancelling her meeting at the last minute."

"There must be something about her you liked. I can't imagine you wasting your time otherwise." Audrey smiled at the waitress who took their order. "Can I get some cream, sweetie?"

The waitress disappeared.

"I was intrigued," he said, speaking a little louder over the rattle of dishes and customer chatter.

"I bet that's what you were," Audrey said. "Intrigued."

"Like when I first heard you sing." He was ready to change the subject. "Speaking of which, we have lots to talk about."

She gave him her already famous smile, and it filled him with hope. He took a lot of satisfaction in the fact that he'd discovered Audrey, and even though she could be demanding, she was on her way up the charts, and fast. His percentage from her music earnings could get the agency back on track in a short time, if he kept her happy and did his job right.

Still smiling, Audrey leaned heavily on the table. "Can I finish at least one cup of coffee before we talk shop? I'm exhausted from the show last night."

"And you were amazing," he said, and meant it. The event had been sold out, and the audience had loved her. It was all good for Audrey and for Adams Music. The business had been struggling ever since he lost his biggest band over a falling-out about money. It always happened that way. Music artists were happy to give their agent a percentage of profits when they were starting out, but when they made it huge, some of them started resenting the agent's cut. Will's policy to that end was to cut those kinds of clients loose, even if it hit his bottom line hard for a while. The problem was, it was still hitting the bottom line hard.

"I used to work here," Audrey said, casting her eyes around the room.

"You never told me that."

She shrugged. "It was just a job. A good job though. June's a peach. Your girl's lucky to have it."

"She's not my girl," he corrected, wishing she were. "And she's not my client, yet." But secretly, Will hoped she'd turn out to be as great as the picture he'd formed in his mind. Gillian had potential as a client. As far as the rest, well, it didn't matter since his clients were off-limits.

Their waitress returned with a small white pitcher.

He looked at Audrey. She was pouting now, and his patience was worn thin. Still, he smiled like a professional.

"What's wrong?"

"Nothing."

He decided to approach the topic with a bit of teasing. "You aren't jealous of Gillian Heart, are you?"

She looked surprised. "Of course not. Why'd I be jealous of a little waitress?" She tipped the pitcher of cream into her coffee.

"Good, because I thought I might introduce you to her sometime."

She narrowed her eyes. "Was her demo really that good?"

"The recording is amateurish, but her voice is amazing."

Audrey set her coffee cup down. "Amazing? Well, can I hear it?"

"Sure, but you're gonna need a CD player."

She looked incredulous. "Old school, huh?"

"So it seems."

"Well you're always saying how you're old school deep down, right? I want to hear her for myself then."

"I was hoping you'd say that. And if you like her,

maybe you could take her under your wing."

"If you sign her."

"Right."

"I'm awfully busy," she said. "But I guess I could do that—for you."

Will looked around for a waitress, ready to eat his late breakfast. He was starving.

"Well now," Audrey said in a sing-song voice. "Isn't this the little songbird waitress you were telling me about, Will?"

Taken aback, he glanced up to see a different waitress: Gillian Heart, holding a coffee pot, her green eyes sparkling and a small smile on her face. Shoot, she was gorgeous.

"Refill?"

"Hello, Ms. Heart. And please." Will leaned back to let her lean in to pour coffee. He noticed she was smaller without high heels, but still on the tall side. He liked that.

"Audrey," he said. "I want you to meet Gillian Heart."

Will was glad to see Audrey offer Gillian a warm smile. "Nice to meet you, Gillian. You been here long, honey? I haven't seen you before."

"Three years," Gillian answered.

"Well, surely you've sang somewhere, besides on that CD Will just told me about."

Will felt a bit sorry for Gillian when her cheeks flushed.

"I'm singing at The Blue Fiddle tonight," she said.

"Will," Audrey said. "We have to go hear this songbird tonight, don't we?"

Will leaned forward on his elbows. "We'll be there."

"Great," Gillian said. She stood, frozen it seemed, for a few long seconds, then her eyes widened. "Oh! I'd better get your food."

Will tried not to watch as she hurried off toward the

kitchen, but he couldn't help noticing the bounce in her step as she disappeared through the curtain.

"She's a doll," Audrey said. Will looked up, hoping his face didn't show the allure he felt toward Gillian Heart.

"She's cute," he said. "I just hope she's good on stage tonight."

"She's more than cute," Audrey said. "Too bad you don't date clients."

He managed to maintain a straight face. Audrey, like everyone in country music, knew about his past. He hadn't done everything that was rumored, but he had dated a client before. Everyone was pretty accepting of the relationship at first, touting them as the new sweethearts of country music, but showbiz took its toll on their relationship. They'd both done stupid things to the other, and the day she'd left Nashville was the day Will had promised himself to never, ever date another client.

"Ah, honey," Audrey said. "You're done for."

Ignoring her, he slurped his coffee, but it wasn't hot enough to burn away his desire to see Gillian again, no matter what his rules, since as soon as she arrived with his meal, he promptly spilled half the coffee in his lap.

"Oh!" she exclaimed, pulling a towel from her waist. "I'm such a klutz today."

"No, it was me," Will said.

She reached like she was going to dab his lap, which made him stiffen and his face flush. She paused, apparently having second thoughts, and handed him the towel. Across from him, Audrey giggled.

"I'll grab some more coffee," Gillian said. He was pretty sure she was fighting a grin as she spun on her heels and strode away.

"Holy crap," he said, dabbing his lap, then slapping the towel onto the table. Audrey was staring at him with that ridiculous smile.

"What?" he demanded, hating that his face still felt warm, which meant he was blushing like a fifteen-year-old boy. "Is something funny?"

She shrugged, her smile only growing broader.

"Like I said, honey. You're done for."

## Chapter Five

Gillian liked how The Blue Fiddle had that historic look typical of honky-tonks on Lower Broadway. She and Tasha had both landed a job there working nights, and between there and The Sweetest Tea, they managed to pay rent. But the best part about working at The Blue Fiddle was the chance to sing in front of a real audience. Tonight was Gillian's night.

Wishing she hadn't eaten that piece of meatloaf for lunch, she lay her apron on the bar and headed toward the stage. Just as she reached for her guitar, Will walked in. Her heart leapt when he smiled and gave her a little salute. Audrey followed close behind, and the two found a table toward the back. Gillian had the distinct feeling she needed to impress Audrey as much as Will. For a moment, she fiddled with the strap on her guitar and strummed a few chords. She was stalling, having tuned her guitar earlier.

Someone clapped. "Let's hear it, sugar!" Gillian thought it was Tasha.

Her stomach fluttered. It didn't get much better for someone like her to stand on the wood planks of that low stage, the window lit with neon signs behind her, the dance floor framed by the long, shiny oak bar, and the rustic brick walls lined with autographed photos and a mismatched collection of fiddles.

She smiled at the crowd, hoping for a panicked split second that nothing was hanging from her nose. At least her outfit looked better than both of the ones Will had seen earlier that day. Tonight, she was all country, dressed in her favorite jeans with the rhinestone pockets, the same boots she'd been wearing back when she first stepped off the bus, and a simple thin-strapped pink blouse that flowed just past her waist. Her hair was down and her makeup no longer dramatic, although she wore darker lipstick because of the dim lighting.

"Ladies and gentlemen, please welcome the beautiful and talented Miss Gillian Heart!"

The lights dimmed, and a lone spotlight curved on the floor in front of her. She was unable to make out the faces just outside the light, but she knew they were there as she crooned her favorite Patsy Cline song, *Crazy*. She knew it was another cliché, like everything else she'd done since she'd arrived in the city, but everyone in Nashville loves Patsy. Besides, it was appropriate for this moment. She felt like she'd go crazy if Will decided to sign her.

Taking a calming breath like her momma taught her, she waited for the room to fade away in her mind until it was just her, the stage and the echoes of Patsy, Loretta and all the other country women who'd paved the way for her. Yes, *for me*, she thought. That's what she told herself every night, to keep from giving up. And she sang.

She sang her heart out, not sure if she sounded any good at all, but praying she did. Finally, she strummed the last chord, eyes closed, and for several seconds there wasn't a sound in the room, not even from the bar.

Had she been flat?

Then a slow, loud clap came from the back of the room, and the rest of the crowd joined in. Hoots and hollers begged for more, so she sang them two additional songs. It was all she was allowed to do before the *real* act came out.

After her last song, there was more applause, accompanied by groans of disappointment when the audience saw her setting her guitar in its stand. She gave people a few minutes to come up to the stage and talk with her, surreptitiously scanning the crowd for Will. Several people passed by the stage, pulling bills from their pockets and stuffing them in the tip jar, or offering a word of praise, but no Will Adams.

"Wow," she said to Tasha when they counted out the bills.

"You deserve it, girl."

"I'm going to buy us dinner," Gillian said. "After we pay rent."

"You don't have to do that," Tasha said.

"I do, because I'm sick of macaroni and cheese."

Some days, she was never gladder to be in Nashville, but there were times when she felt like hanging up her hat and going back to Gold Creek Gap, where her momma would make her a real meal and she'd have a comfortable mattress. Even her dinky twin bed in Momma's little trailer house was more comfortable than the creaky box springs in her apartment.

The bartender called to Gillian. "Hey, Patsy, I need you to take tables six through ten tonight, OK?"

"Why?" She caught a sad look from Tasha.

"Because Jenny's gone."

"Gone where?" Gillian asked in a lowered voice when she passed Tasha carrying a full tray of drinks.

"Poor thing went home. She ran out of money and probably out of willpower too." Tasha didn't say she gave up, because everyone there understood the hardship of trying to make it in Nashville.

"But I liked Jenny."

"Yeah, me too, but who can blame her?" Tasha asked. "Don't *you* ever think about leaving?"

"Sometimes." Gillian couldn't lie. She'd just been thinking about home, but she wasn't ready to go home permanently. "Do you?"

"Yeah, every damn day."

"But you're still here."

Tasha shrugged. "And so are you."

Gillian had promised her mom, and herself, that she'd give it plenty of time, and she wasn't ready to go back to teaching small town guitar lessons to little kids and singing in the church choir. Not that she didn't enjoy those things, but her dreams were bigger than Gold Creek Gap. And that's why she hoped tonight might be her big break. She scanned the room, looking for Will Adams. Her gaze rested on the back table.

A small earthquake rumbled in Gillian's chest. "Do you see him?"

"Who doesn't?" Tasha asked, moving off to deliver her drinks.

Will and Audrey sat at one of her assigned tables, so taking a deep breath, she headed their way. He was sitting with his lanky legs sheathed in expensive-looking jeans and boots stretched out in front of him. His gaze scanned the room and landed on her as she approached. He smiled, sending Gillian's heart into a frenzy.

The man radiated masculinity by doing nothing at all. Be professional, she reminded herself, but dang, he was attractive with that slightly scruffy look of his. His pepper-streaked blond hair was just long enough to be disheveled, but short enough to be professional in a country-music sort of way, and no skinny jeans, thank heavens. His black starched shirt with its pearl snap buttons down the front was loose, as if he'd untucked it after a long day, and his black western boots had lost some of the shine Gillian fancied must have been there that morning. She knew Will's type. He was a workaholic to be sure, but that was probably why he was one of the best.

"Hey," she said, forcing herself to turn and look at Audrey. "Hi, Audrey. Thanks, both of you, for coming."

"Darlin'," Will said, "can you please do that again?"

Gillian's pulse rushed a lot faster than it should have when he rested his elbows on the table to peer at her, the intense blue of his eyes drawing her in, her heart fluttering and completely oblivious to the warning signals in her brain.

"What he means," Audrey said, "is that you have a great voice."

A flush of pride spread across her cheeks, igniting a flame of hope for her music career, along with a heat wave of a different kind that swept through her body. The last part, she chose to ignore.

Be professional, she reminded herself again, but what she really wanted to do was flirt.

"Nice of you to say," Gillian said, attempting to sound normal. "What will the two of you have to drink?"

"He'll have a beer, and I'll have a deluxe margarita on the rocks—on his tab." Audrey winked at Gillian.

"I'll be right back." She turned, but stopped when she felt Will's hand on her arm.

"Please call Josie first thing in the morning. I can't wait for lunch. We need to talk soon."

Letting go of her, he pulled out his card and asked for a pen. Her hands were shaking, but she managed to hand him one.

"If Josie doesn't answer, call this number. It's my

personal cell."

Gillian flushed when she noted Audrey's raised eyebrows.

"Congratulations, honey," Audrey said. "Not everyone gets Will's private cell."

"Thank you," Gillian said, doing her best not to clutch the card to her chest and do a happy dance. "Thank you so much."

"You have a beautiful voice," Audrey said. "I'm almost jealous."

"I'll be right back with your drinks." She rushed back to the bar where Tasha was waiting.

"Well?"

"I'm supposed to go into his office tomorrow."

Tasha grabbed her hands. The two squealed.

∽∾

When Gillian delivered the drinks, a new person was with them.

"Gillian, meet Mitch Brewster. He's another music agent." She had heard of him.

"Gorgeous voice," he said. "And you, you are beautiful." Gillian gave him a bemused look. Mitch was already half lit.

"What can I get you?" she asked.

He rattled off his order and then handed Gillian his business card. Will Adams gave his buddy a friendly punch in the shoulder.

"Mitch, you can't sign this girl."

"Why? She's amazing."

"I found her first," Will said. Gillian glanced at Audrey, who was simply shaking her head.

"Ignore them both," Audrey said. "Sign with who you want to. Just remember, they're going to be working for you." She cast a meaningful look from Mitch to Will.

"Sign with me," Mitch said. He grabbed her free hand, wrapping his sweaty fingers around hers. "Where'd you get those pipes anyway, sugar?"

Gillian had always heard that gentlemen were everywhere in country music, but when she actually got to Nashville and started waiting tables, it didn't take long to learn that jerks were everywhere, even in country music.

She pulled her hand free. "Just give me a beer, sweetheart. We can talk when you get back." He rested his hand low on Gillian's hip. She was about to whip him with her towel when Will Adams' hand shot out and grabbed his friend by the wrist.

"That's no way to treat a lady, Mitch." He smiled apologetically at Gillian. "Sorry about that. Bring him a coffee, please. He's already drunk. It's been a long day for both of us."

That man was the reason she didn't date men in Nashville any more. So many of them were either cads, or they were off-limits, like Will Adams. She'd learned the hard way from seeing her dad leave her mom—and her—not to get attached to music people. But good gravy, Will Adams was the kind of man who might change her mind.

As she approached the bar, she rattled off the Mitch guy's order and waited for the bartender to fill a cup with coffee.

"I'm sorry about my friend."

She whirled around to see Will, standing close to the bar. The attraction crackled like the static electricity in her grade school science experiment. It left her feeling restless. She felt like yanking her apron off and pulling Will Adams out onto the dance floor.

"You can really sing."

Gillian suddenly understood why women swooned in old romantic movies. His smile made her feel light-headed.

"Thank you." She picked up the coffee.

"I'll take that to Mitch," Will said.

"Thanks," she said, grateful.

"Until tomorrow," he said, grinning. She added his eyes to the growing list of things she would have to resist about him if he became her agent.

"Tomorrow," she said, pretending to be calm, even though she was trembling all over.

He smiled, and she got the feeling he was thinking similar thoughts. If they signed together, they might never get a chance to explore the sparks between them.

"You two are hot," Tasha said.

Gillian grinned. "I think I agree, but I want a record deal, not sparks."

"You clearly want more than sparks with Will Adams," she teased. "It's totally obvious."

Gillian thought Tasha was right, though sparks rarely led to anything but getting burned, which she had experienced first-hand. When she finally did find the right man, she'd want even more than sparks. The truth? She wanted love, but she wanted her music career first. And when love finally happened, she didn't want it with someone like Will Adams, no matter how he rocked her to her core.

❧

Will handed Mitch the coffee and sat next to Audrey.

"She's gonna be hot," Audrey said.

*She already is* were the words on the tip of his tongue as he remembered the sweet scent of her perfume and the lingering aroma of sweetened coffee on her breath.

"She's gonna be amazing, as long as we can sign her before these other bastards get to her." His gaze moved from Mitch to a half dozen other music business people he knew around the room. He had a mind to stay and make sure nobody else got to talk to her, but it wasn't his way to be desperate. Will knew exactly how to seduce a woman, but he'd learned there was a fine balance between showing eagerness and neutrality when seducing a client.

He just wished he could do both.

## Chapter Six

Will accepted a steaming cup of coffee from Josie.

"Thanks. Did you get a phone call from Gillian Heart?"

"Not yet."

"When you do, can you send her through?"

"I sure will." Will thought he saw a small smile on Josie's face as she shuffled back to her desk. He softly closed the door to his office, then typed Gillian's name into his web browser. He didn't usually troll for singers online, but he had a short list of bookmarked sites for when he did. Gillian Heart's bio popped up on all of them. It described her as a small town girl from Gold Creek Gap. He rubbed his chin stubble.

Heart. Of course.

He leaned back in his chair. "Well, I'll be dogged. She is his daughter after all."

Leaning forward again, the chair squeaking under his weight, he clicked on a picture of Gillian Heart. She was posed in a country setting, possibly Gold Creek Gap, leaning against a rustic wooden fence post. Her green eyes peered from beneath a western straw hat, and her long hair cascaded around her shoulders, with a sleeveless blue top peeking through the strands. She wore a pair of jeans and those same boots she'd been wearing at The Blue Fiddle. He wondered if they were her favorites, or the only boots she owned.

When Josie transferred the call, he was expecting her.

"Gillian Heart."

"Hi," she said, sounding unsure.

"I wondered if you were ever gonna call," he said.

There was a beat of silence. "You seem like such a busy person," she said. "I didn't want to presume."

"Lesson one. If someone important gives you their number, call them as soon as possible."

"Are you saying you're important?" Her voice held a hint of playfulness that surprised him.

"I want you to come in," he said.

"When?"

"The sooner the better."

"I'm free today."

"I am too. One o'clock?"

"OK."

"And Gillian?"

"Yes?"

"Bring that guitar of yours."

៚

Will automatically stood when Gillian Heart, dressed in blue jeans, boots and a red long-sleeved western shirt, stepped into his office. Her shirt was modest, downright chaste compared to what she'd worn when they'd bumped into each other the morning before, but no less sexy on her. He liked how the color set off the creamy skin of her cheeks.

"I'm glad you came," he said, pulling out a leather chair. He was careful not to touch her as she sat down, even though he would have liked to lay a hand on her shoulder. She had an obvious case of the jitters that were making her hands shake.

"I was afraid you might change your mind." He took his own seat on the opposite side of the desk facing her.

"I wanted to come," she said, offering him a nervous smile. He noted her glance at the collection of photographs and awards. The pictures of him with his top clients were his résumé, and they were displayed to impress music artists he was hoping to sign, like Gillian Heart. He gave her a moment to study them while he studied her.

She was star material, but she wasn't the kind to know it, and that could be wildly attractive to an audience, never mind to him. The night before, Audrey had remarked about her small town quality. He was from a small town too, and he was struck with the thought that his sisters, who still lived there, would love her.

Eventually, Gillian's gaze shifted to the large window that framed an impressive view of Music Row, where all the best music agents had offices. It was a prime piece of real estate in Nashville, and he'd been lucky to have bought it from a retiring agency years earlier after receiving the biggest songwriting paycheck in his life. He'd had to split it with Heart, the guy he assumed was Gillian's dad, but there was plenty left over.

"So, Gillian. Tell me a little about yourself."

She launched into a speech that was verbatim from the website, reminding him of a kid about to perform in a local talent show. It was cute, but they'd need to work on presentation when she wasn't singing.

"I mostly learned to sing in church," she said. "I know it's cliché, but my momma taught me to play guitar, and I taught myself to play the banjo. I learned the violin in fifth grade, but when I was supposed to be practicing sonatas, I was practicing *Wabash Cannonball.*"

"I guess I like clichés," he said. She gave him an easy smile, but he noted her clenched hands. "Lots of country musicians first cut their teeth on small town church music. Especially here in the South."

She nodded. She was very short on words.

"That's how I first fell in love with country music myself," he said.

She looked surprised. "You? In church?"

He laughed out loud, which made her smile a little wider.

"You can't always judge a book—or a record album—by the cover," he said. "I don't make it back much, but I'm from a small town."

"That's cool," she said.

"How about you? Do you ever get back to Gold Creek Gap?" He wanted to ask her about her dad, wondering why she hadn't mentioned him herself. Most folks would be quick to offer any connection they already had in a business where connections were often a way to get noticed.

"A few times a year to see my momma."

"And your dad?"

Her eyes darkened. "He's not in the picture."

Will could see he needed to be careful, so he made his voice as matter of fact as possible. "But he's in the music business, right?"

He hadn't meant to be pushy, but the agent in him needed to know anything that could help him get her a record deal.

She gave him an indecisive stare, then a light seemed to dawn in her eyes before darkening back into a gray cloud.

"You mean Cooper Heart?"

He grinned. "Cooper Heart."

"You've heard of him, then."

"Of course. Who in country music hasn't? At first I didn't make the connection, but then I thought I remembered he was from Gold Creek Gap. I did a quick Internet search and sure enough, he is."

"He was," she said.

Will didn't bother to probe into the relationship. He knew Cooper Heart only as a songwriter. Cooper kept his personal life close to the vest any time Will worked with him. It didn't matter anyway. Will was interested in the connection for other purposes.

"How is he?"

"I wouldn't know."

He nodded. "If you'd mentioned him sooner, I would've cancelled everything to meet with you right away. Musical gifts often flow from generation to generation, and your dad has written dozens of hits. But you already know that."

She narrowed her eyelids. "Trust me. I got my talent from my momma."

"She writes too?"

Gillian nodded. "And sings like a dream."

"So you have it from both sides. You know, I'm surprised your dad didn't call me about you coming in. For that matter, he could've brought you in himself. He in town?"

She shrugged. "I wouldn't know, but it doesn't matter. I can make my own way."

He nodded. That was an odd thing for a daughter to say about her father. He made a mental note to check on what else Cooper Heart had been up to in the past decade, just to see if there were any skeletons Will might have to work with—or that might work for him—if he got Gillian Heart to let him represent her.

"Listen. Your story's important. You're the daughter of a single mom, you're from a small town, your dad left when you were a little girl, and he just happens to be this great Nashville connection. And yet, you are here all on your own, without him, trying to make it. Record labels are going to love that. Your fans are going to want the whole package, and you've got it."

"What's the whole package?"

He chuckled. Apparently bringing up her father had made her a little feisty.

"For starters," he said, "you're gorgeous." She *was* a knockout, and he enjoyed being able to tell her so with his agent hat on, even though it made her cheeks blush deeper. "You also have a good story, even though I can see it makes you uncomfortable to talk about it. But most importantly you *can* sing."

She smiled, looking a bit dazed, and he decided not to press her any further about Cooper Heart right then.

"So," he said, motioning to her guitar case. "Why don't you sing for me right now?"

"Um. OK. What should I play?"

"Anything at all, darlin'."

It didn't take her long to get settled before she started picking out a rhythm, accompanied by the haunting lyrics of a love song with a bluegrass feel. He was heady with excitement about the way it fit her story, her personality and the sweet Southern voice spilling out of her mouth like honey. He was surely in love—at least with her voice—and that, thank the good Lord, was allowed.

"And then there's this." She launched into a song he instinctively knew would make people want to sing along. When she finished, he felt himself grinning like a Cheshire cat.

"Dang, girl. You wrote all these yourself?"

"Yep."

"Sing me another."

She obliged, and his body involuntarily kept time with the music, nodding with the beat, tapping and slapping.

At The Blue Fiddle he'd only heard her sing Patsy Cline songs, and they were good, but these songs made his pulse race, and for once it wasn't only because of how pretty she was. Looks might help a singer's career, but talent secured it. Gillian could sing and write, and she had a breezy acoustic feel that record companies would love. She strummed the last note, letting it resonate through his office, before slapping her hand down on the strings.

For a few seconds Will could only stare.

"What?" The Southern drawl in her voice was a little thicker from being so freshly lost in her songs. He shook his head, in love with every song she sang.

"Do you play anything besides that guitar, the banjo and the fiddle?" As if that weren't already enough.

"The mandolin, and of course, the piano."

"Of course you do." She was Cooper Heart's daughter, but he wasn't about to say it out loud after her earlier response to his mentioning the name. It was rare for artists to walk into his office and sing their own story in a way that was so authentically part of their roots, and at the same time, a reflection of the newer, more progressive sound in country music. If he could get her to sign with him, he'd do everything he could to protect that sound.

She wriggled under his gaze. "Did you like it?"

"Darlin', I'm in love." He thoroughly enjoyed seeing her melt under his praise. "If you keep doing that, I'm gonna marry you on the spot."

Smiling, she stared down at her guitar, strumming a few chords. He'd been kidding, but a flash of her all in white wasn't an unpleasant picture. It filled him with a sentimentality that shocked him. He'd never been a romantic before, not when it came to his future.

She smiled. "Are you proposing?"

So she did have some spunk underneath that shyness.

He didn't miss a beat. "There *is* a Vegas-style chapel down the road. It's Elvis-themed, if you're into that."

"Now *that* would be crazy," she said, laughing.

He laughed too. What a crazy thought. But watching her slim shoulders shake with laughter, he thought it wouldn't be too crazy in a different situation in which he was free to pursue her as a woman instead of as a client. He sighed. That was never gonna happen. He'd been there, done that, with someone else once, and it'd been a disaster in which everyone involved was hurt, but especially the girl. He ignored the guilty pang in his heart. He'd never been anything but bad for women, especially the good ones.

"Then will you at least let me rep you?" he asked, shifting to the serious face he used for business deals.

Her giggles stopped, and a look of mild surprise passed over her features, as if his proposing to represent her was crazier than his pretend marriage proposal.

The heck if she doesn't blush again, he mused.

He hoped she wouldn't turn red on stage every time she performed, but in the privacy of his office, he found it charming. In fact, it made him want to touch her cheek, kiss that sweet mouth of hers until all her fears were gone.

"What do you say?" he asked, mentally straightening his music manager hat. "Can I be your agent?"

"You want me that badly?" she asked. He could tell she was being sincere, nothing but music on her mind.

"Yes, I definitely want you." It was all he could do to keep a straight face, his mind on just the music. It wasn't an easy task when she embodied all the things he *would* love in a woman, if he were to ever fall in love with one again.

"Well then, yes," she said. "I'd be honored."

"You would?" He wondered if she realized she was good enough to get any agent in Nashville if she worked on her presentation and told people she was Heart's daughter. Most agents didn't have time for shy, mousy girls, but surely those other agents had been impressed with her at The Blue Fiddle. Lord have mercy. He should have some competition.

"You'll let me rep you then?"

"Sure I will. I need to cancel a few appointments first. A few agents approached me last night, and I scheduled appointments with them, just in case."

"Of course they did." Will felt a wave of jealousy. "Just tell Josie who they were, and she'll cancel them for you."

She nodded.

"OK," he said, leaping up like a spring and reaching across the desk for her hand. They shook on it, and his mind was running a million directions at once.

"We have a lot of planning to do," he said. "I don't know about you, but I'm starving. You still available for lunch?"

"Sure," she said, grinning. "But no sushi."

# Chapter Seven

Gillian hated the messy scrawl that was supposed to be her signature as she scratched the pen across the bottom of her contract with Adams Music Management, but it would do. It'd only been a few days since her meeting with Will, and just like that, after three years in Nashville, she had a music agent.

Gillian couldn't wait to call her momma. She'd be over the moon with happiness. Gillian had hoped and prayed she'd accomplish her dreams of being a singer, not only for herself, but for her momma—and this was the biggest step so far. For a sentimental instant, she thought of her dad too. Last she'd heard of him, he was spending the majority of his time on some island in the Caribbean with one of his girlfriends, limiting his time in Nashville to a few months a year. The chances she'd ever run into him again were slim to none. And it was a good thing, she reminded herself. She never wanted to see him again.

"Congratulations." Will drew her back to the present.

He held the contract up for Josie who was holding a camera, a friendly smile on her face.

"Welcome to the Adams Family," Josie said, a wry look on her face. As corny as it was, it made Gillian laugh. There was a click and a flash, forever capturing Will's confident grin and Gillian's dazed is-this-really-happening smile.

❧

"I guess that necklace you gave me finally brought some luck," she told Momma over the phone.

"Honey, that necklace isn't lucky. You signed that contract because you worked hard and you deserve it. Will Adams is a smart man to get you to sign with him."

"He didn't have to try that hard."

"Don't you ever tell him that, honey."

Gillian smiled, imagining the tough look her momma would have on her face right at that moment if she could see her.

"OK. I won't."

"I miss you, baby."

The homesickness hit Gillian like a train. She choked back a sob. "I miss you too, Momma."

"Baby, be strong. It's all coming together."

"I know," Gillian said. "So tell me, what's new in Gold Creek Gap?"

Her mom laughed. "Honey, nothing is ever new here."

"Good," Gillian said. "Tell me about it."

"Honey, are you really that homesick?"

"Yes."

"Oh, baby." She cleared her throat, and Gillian knew that, like her, Momma was holding back her own tears.

"All right," Momma said. "Melanie had another baby."

"She did? Oh my goodness. A boy or a girl?" Melanie was her cousin and had been her best friend growing up. But they hadn't been in touch much since Gillian moved to Nashville.

"Girl. She named her Sheyenne."

"Really? I love it. We can call her Shey."

"That's what I told her." As Gillian curled up on her bed, she pulled close the quilt her momma had made and listened as she rattled on about all the news and gossip. When she started yawning, her momma heard and said she had to go.

"I'll visit soon," Gillian said.

"Don't you dare do that. I'll come see you instead, as soon as I can take some time off work, OK?"

"But it's not the same here. It's busy and noisy."

"Pretty soon, you're going to be too busy to be homesick."

Gillian doubted anything could take her mind off all of the things she missed about home, but she'd throw herself into her music anyway. If her career took off, she'd have enough money to go back and forth between Nashville and Gold Creek Gap as much as she wanted, and unlike her no-good dad, she'd never stop going back to see Momma.

෨ළ

"I hope you're ready for your first big gig," Will said. They were ordering at a little coffee shop within walking distance of her and Tasha's apartment. One thing she'd learned about Will is he wasn't one to sit in his office all day. It wasn't unusual for him to be meeting with clients and record executives in coffee shops, restaurants and even on the golf course. She drew the line at the golf course.

"You should go with me some time," he told her.

"No thanks. Nobody in Gold Creek Gap golfs, so I never learned."

"I grew up in a small town too," he said. "And now I can play mediocre par."

"Is that good?"

"It's mediocre," he said with a chuckle. "One stroke over par on every hole."

"Hmm. Maybe someday," Gillian said. "If you'll stop trying to get me to eat sushi."

He laughed. "I'm never going to stop trying to get you to like sushi."

Still dressed in a white collared polo style shirt and a pair of khaki shorts, he looked adorable, even if she preferred his boots.

"What? You don't golf in boots?" she asked.

"Only because they won't let me." He carried their drinks to a corner table near the window.

"So where's my first big gig?"

"The Steel Spur."

She set her coffee down abruptly, causing the lid to pop off. It was only the biggest place for an up-and-coming music artist to perform in Nashville, besides The Wild Horse Saloon and the Ryman, of course.

"Holy cow, Will. I don't know if I'm ready for that. I mean, I just signed. Don't I need some kind of grooming or training or something?"

"I have a girl who'll help you with your hair, maybe some of those highlights and stuff, some new jeans that you can pay the agency back for later. That kind of thing, but mostly, I want you to be the small town girl I saw at The Blue Fiddle."

She'd been hoping he'd get her a giant makeover with someone who knew what they were doing, something to get rid of the small town in her. And pay the agency back? The mere thought of it made her sick to her stomach. It'd be a long time before she'd have enough money for that, but she'd pay every penny when she could.

"Why do you want me to be a small town girl? Maybe I came here to get away from all that."

◦◦◦

Will smiled, knowing she'd never get away from all that. Heaven knows, he'd tried himself, and his own small town upbringing remained deeply embedded no matter how long he'd lived in Nashville. One thing he loved about Gillian's personality was that she was so unaware of how endearing the whole small town thing was, not only to him, but to an audience.

"I like small town girls," he said. "I came from a small town, remember?"

"When's the last time you went back?"

Her question hit him square in the heart. His mom had asked him the same question the night before on the phone. He called her once a week, no fail, and she always asked the same question. He needed to visit soon. He was always intending to, but he was just so busy. Of course, his parents didn't understand that, especially his mom.

"It's been about a year." He waited for her to express shock, but instead, a sadness passed over her face.

"Same for me," she said. "I used to go home a few times a year, but money's been tight." He didn't say anything but noted the way her shoulders slumped.

"Homesick much?"

"Every day."

"The best way to handle being homesick is to remember why you're here," he said. "Why are you here?"

She wrinkled her forehead. "To get a record deal."

"And who are you doing it for?"

"My momma."

He nodded. He believed her. And that was another one of the things he enjoyed about her. She was all about family, even though hers lived far away, and it gave her a softness that other women in Nashville didn't always have, at least not the kind he hung out with.

"Your momma did a good job with you. I bet she's proud. Are you her only kid?"

"That's me," she said. "A lonely only child."

She'd told him she didn't want kids until she'd made it big, but that once she did, she wanted a bunch of them. Her comment had sent little swirls through his stomach that made him feel completely ridiculous. He could see her as a mother, but she was right about her career. He hoped she wouldn't meet some guy who swept her off her feet and convinced her to have a family before he could get her career going. In fact, he hoped she didn't meet a man at all.

"I hope you're doing this whole music thing for yourself too."

"Of course."

"And your dad?" He figured it was worth a try to get her to talk about him.

"Listen," she said. "I don't mean to be rude. I know you've heard of my dad, and he's probably some kind of inspiration to you with all the hit songs he's written, but I don't have a relationship with him. I don't want a relationship with him."

He leaned on his elbows, trying to gauge how serious she was.

"Darlin'," he said, hating to push, but he had to. "I really want to use that angle. You don't have to have a relationship with him in order to say you're his daughter. I guarantee it's going to help."

Her cheeks reddened, deepening in color down her neck and across the fine skin along her collar. He felt horrible, but this was business. Connections wouldn't make her career, but they could open doors.

"I'm not his daughter," she said, her tone as vicious as he figured she could ever sound. "Dads visit their daughters. They don't forget about them."

He reached across the table and lay a hand softly on her wrist, the feel of it rousing a desire to pull her into his arms and smooth her pain away.

"I'm sorry. I didn't mean to upset you."

She shook her head. "It's not you. It's him." Her voice softened. "It's just that if he can't claim me, I'm not claiming him."

He sighed, not seeing any way he could convince her of how publicly naming her father would open doors for her in Nashville. Clients didn't always know the best way to promote themselves. That's why they had him.

"Just think about this," he said. "People will find out anyway. It's not like you've changed your last name, right?"

She shrugged. Will glanced across the table at her. She definitely resembled her father, especially when she was being stubborn. Then he thought back to Gillian's words about Cooper Heart. She was right: Cooper Heart had been an inspiration to Will in those early days. Will had thought Cooper was a great guy, but he must have been wrong. He now thought that when he saw Cooper again, which could be any time in Nashville, he'd be the first to tell him he was crazy to have abandoned Gillian.

"As your agent, I suggest you say you are his daughter early in your career. That way, you have control. Send out a tweet. Facebook it, if you want."

She shook her head brusquely. "I'm not changing my mind."

Maybe, he thought, she'd change her mind in the long run, but when he glanced at the determined angle of her slender jaw, he wasn't so sure. He'd keep the Cooper

Heart card in his back pocket and only use it if he needed to push hard to get her a record deal.

"About The Steel Spur," he said. Her face brightened, and he was glad to see her happy again. "Audrey volunteered to listen to you rehearse, to give you some pointers."

"Sure. I'd appreciate that."

"I trust her opinion," he said. "You should too. The Steel Spur's a huge opportunity, and you want to be ready."

"I know." She sat up straighter. "I'll do my best."

"You'll do great," he said.

"Do you think they'll like my songs?"

"Darlin', trust me. It don't matter what you sing. They won't be able to get your voice, or your pretty face, off their minds."

Just like me, he thought.

# Chapter Eight

Where The Blue Fiddle was quaint with its regular honky-tonk crowd and cozy atmosphere, The Steel Spur was all lights and plenty of action. On any given night it was packed with tourists and locals alike, and the only acts they let on were the best and surely headed for the charts. Gillian could hardly believe she was getting to perform!

"Heavens to Betsy," she said. "I'm so nervous." As she waited behind the curtains, Will placed a hand on the small of her back. She took a deep breath.

"You'll do fine."

She drew strength from the pressure of his hands as they massaged up her back and gripped her shoulders.

"You've worked hard for this, darlin'."

"You're going to have to stop calling me darlin'," she teased, just to get her mind off her butterflies. Maybe it was the way he leaned in close enough that she could smell his cologne, but she remembered something Audrey had said to her one day as she was going over her set. Audrey had been giving her pointers about the music, but she'd also been giving her some other tips.

"Don't do anything to invite gossip," Audrey had said, her face serious. Gillian wondered if Audrey thought she had dibs on Will or something.

Audrey must have read her mind because she'd laughed. "Heavens no, doll. It's not that way between Will and me. I've got a man."

Gillian had been unable to explain her relief.

"Look, all I'm saying," Audrey said, "is that neither of you need this town gossiping about your love lives. He's been through the wringer already, and while he's obviously hot for you, doll, he doesn't date clients—any more."

"OK," Gillian had told her, but after that, she kept thinking about what Audrey had said about Will being obviously hot for her. Was it that obvious? And was it the other way around too? Could people see she was hot for him? The idea made her smile a bit, when it probably should have made her afraid. The tabloids could be relentless.

"I'll call you darlin' if I want," he said. "As long as it's OK with you."

"It is," she said. "But people might think there's more between us than agent and client." She was no longer teasing.

When he didn't say anything, she turned slightly to look at him. His eyes were intent on her in the dim light.

"Would that be so bad?" His voice was quiet in her ear.

She wasn't sure what to say. Yes. No, of course not. Yes. Heck no, that would be unprofessional. And yes. A million times yes. He must have mistaken her silence for an answer.

"Never mind," he said. "I shouldn't have said that."

Then, Gillian heard the announcer say her name.

"Go." He gave her a soft nudge. "You're gonna be a hit, darlin'."

Gillian walked into the spotlight, her trusty boots grounding her into the wooden stage. She stood on the bit of orange tape marking her spot. Will had suggested over and over that she needed a new pair of boots, but she wanted to wear her own. She hadn't told Will they were a gift from her dad. It would've sounded crazy after she'd ranted about wanting nothing to do with him. And she didn't, but that didn't mean she couldn't miss him, wish he was there or hold memories of him in her heart.

She'd worn those boots since she was thirteen, singing the national anthem at dozens of rodeos, *Amazing Grace* in front of churches and Patsy Cline songs in her share of talent competitions. They still fit, and it seemed right to be wearing them at her first big gig, along with the necklace from her momma.

The big lights blinded her as she cleared her throat and strummed a chord. She wished she could make out the faces of her friends who promised to be there, but it was impossible. Even Tasha's bossy countenance would have been reassuring.

Realizing the silence was because everyone was waiting on her, she leaned into the mic and said hello. It came out as a croak, and the microphone crackled. The lights dimmed, and her eyes adjusted a little. A few good-natured chuckles come from the people seated at the numerous tables. Several folks were leaning on the railings from the balcony.

"Whooo, Gillian!" The shout broke the strangling silence. Recognizing Tasha's exuberant voice, she found herself cracking a smile.

"I'm pretty sure that was my roommate," she said, her voice rising in the microphone. "We've got rent to pay, so I'd better get singin'."

Laughter and mild applause rippled through the

crowd. With that welcoming reverberation, she leaned closer to the microphone and crooned the first few stanzas of a song, acapella, drawing it out long and soft before strumming her guitar and launching into the melody. Behind her, The Steel Spur band followed along, the banjo and fiddle players picking out the sounds she herself had written. The place was alive with music and her own voice, and as the pace picked up, couples began to fill the wide, shining dance floor.

With each song, the crowd reacted enthusiastically, which was so much more than she'd hoped for. After the last song, applause thundered off the walls.

"Goodnight, y'all!" She waved at them.

The crowd responded with whistles and hollers, and she had to keep reminding herself they were cheering for her. When she came off the stage, Will spun her around and pushed her right back out.

"What the heck?"

"They want the encore, darlin'."

She walked back up to the microphone and rearranged her guitar. Leaning toward the mic, she realized this was the first time she'd ever really felt at one with a crowd.

"I guess y'all want one more song."

"We want ten," called some cowboy from the back of the room.

"Well," she said. "There's another act after me, but I do have one more for y'all. This one's my happy song."

It was a silly little song she'd written with her dad when she was only thirteen, not too long before he left and she'd started writing about broken hearts. She hadn't played it for anyone before, so the band had to catch up with her, but when they did, it was amazing, and she had to admit, she really felt happy in the moment.

When she finally exited the stage, Will reached for her, and the intimacy of it caused musical notes to waltz around in her stomach.

"I'm so proud of you." He enveloped her in his arms. She couldn't find it in herself to resist him as he gently pulled her against the solidness of his chest, nor could she rid herself of the thought that maybe holding women in his arms was something he did often. Now that was a ridiculous thought, she realized. She had no reason to think of—or care about—his dating or how many women he'd held. He was simply her manager.

And yet, in her heart she knew he wasn't. One thing was for sure though, he was certainly good at holding a girl in a way that made her want to throw her arms around his neck. The singer part of her didn't give a hoot who else he'd held, but she realized with a start that the woman side of her did.

"Do you do this to Audrey when she comes off stage?"

"She'd slap my face."

Gillian chuckled. "I was nervous out there."

"You crushed it." Suddenly he was crushing her to his chest in a bear hug. She laughed, gently extricating herself, even though she didn't mind being pressed up against him. Not one little bit.

"Thank you," she said. "For tonight, for getting me here, for signing me, for… everything."

Before she could think about what she was doing, she stretched up on the tiptoes of her boots, plunged one hand through that thick mop of his hair, and planted a kiss on his cheek. She ached to kiss him firmly on the mouth, but truth be known, she wished he'd kiss her first, even if he was her music manager. He seemed to be about to, until a sharp voice penetrated the spell.

"Will Adams." The Steel Spur's manager was headed their way with his hand stretched out. Will shook it enthusiastically, and then it was Gillian's turn.

"What have I done to deserve an act like you, sugar?"

Gillian shrugged, deciding to dismiss the fact that even though she was a grown woman whom he didn't even know, he'd just referred to her as something used in cakes, cookies and to sweeten one's coffee. Deciding he was being sincere, she smiled primly.

"You must have been a very good boy?"

Will smiled approvingly as the man exploded into laughter. "I want you to come back. We'd like to have more of what we saw tonight."

"Any time," Will answered for her. "Call me, and we'll set it up."

The two men shook on it, then Will took her hand and placed it in the crook of his arm, walking her to the stage exit and past the dance floor.

"I can handle everything from here on out. Any time anyone asks you something like that, just defer to me."

She shook her head in disbelief. "I don't know if I'm ever going to get used to having an agent."

"You probably won't, but you'll learn to deal with it."

"Gillian!" Tasha and as many of her friends who could get off work grabbed her arms and ushered her back to a table they'd reserved. They toasted her with clinks and chugs, making Gillian an emotional wreck. How did she get so lucky?

"You have a lot of good friends." Will scanned the group of supporters. Gillian noted that they were all overly polite to Will. They were no doubt nervous about who he was, but they warmed up to him. Soon several of them broke off to hit the dance floor.

She liked hanging out with Will like this, seeing him relaxed and jovial, not working. "Are you having fun?"

"Me? Oh yeah. But this night is about you. Are you having fun?"

"I'd be having more fun if I were out there."

"Then how about a dance, darlin'?" Will held out the crook of his arm. Gillian took it, casting good-natured warning looks to her friends as they whispered and giggled like teenagers.

Out on the dance floor, Will held her at arm's length, even though she wished he'd pull her closer—much closer.

"You're going be a star," he said.

"We'll see," she said.

"It gives them hope, you know." He nodded to the group gathered around the table in the back.

"My friends? Yeah, I guess so."

"That's why they're so happy for you."

He settled in as the lead, his left hand on her hip and his right hand holding hers gently as they began to two-step to the rhythms of The Steel Spur band. Will was good, and she followed his movements like they'd danced together before.

"You like to lead," she said, noting his fluid movement, perfect steps and the sure way he held onto her. His hand rested solidly on her hip, sending little waves of electricity up her torso.

"I do. Especially when I'm dancing with a beautiful woman."

His compliment found its mark, even though she was sure he was the type who said that to all the ladies. She was a pretty good dancer in her own right, and the two of them rocked around the dance floor like they'd been dancing together forever. After the first spin, the band settled into Gillian's favorite Darius Rucker love song, and before she realized it, Will had pulled her close, both hands on her hips, encouraging her to sway in a rhythm with him. It took very little encouragement on her side, and the two of them moved in time together.

He smiled down at her. "You have rhythm."

"I'm a musician."

"It doesn't always translate to dancing." He slowly spun her around and captured her in his arms again.

"That's all in the body."

"You're not so bad yourself," she said.

She caught a tantalizing whiff of his cologne mixed with lingering hints of cigar smoke and the faintest hint of sweat that filled her senses with the manliness of it. That probably would've sounded funny to say, but after living for years with her single mom and then rooming with Tasha, she wasn't accustomed to having a man around. Inhaling the scent of him, she watched the pulse throb in his neck. It felt like such a secret thing to see up close how his blood rushed through his veins. It quickened her own pulse.

He gazed down at her. "Do you dance often?"

"Hardly ever. I'm usually so exhausted after I get off work at night, I go home and binge on Hallmark movies."

"So you're a romantic?" He adjusted his hand comfortably at the curve of her waist. The chills shivering up her arms were impossible to hide. He responded by sliding his hand around the small of her back and pulling her a little bit closer, tucking one of her hands inside of his. Before she could stop it, not that she wanted to, the space between them completely disappeared. She found herself more than enjoying the feel of his body against hers, wishing they could be this way all the time, hating that tomorrow it would probably be back to business again.

"You're beautiful tonight," he whispered. Her pulse raced, and she responded by pressing her cheek against his chest. Feeling the crisp fabric of his western shirt on her face, she found herself inexplicably wishing it were the warmth of his skin instead. He whispered something else that she couldn't hear over the beat of the music, and she lifted her head to hear.

"What did you say?"

She could feel his breath quicken. His palm tightened

around hers, and he pressed her gently back to his chest.

"Nothing." His voice was low in her ear. "I shouldn't have said it."

She burned to hear what it was he shouldn't have said, but before she could insist he repeat it, he pulled her tighter, resting his chin on top of her head.

"It can wait," he said, running one hand lightly up her back and leaning over her, breathing softly into her hair. When the music ended, the two stood for a few beats longer, the electricity drawing them together.

His hands slid up to her face, and he ran a thumb lightly along her jaw. "Lord have mercy, woman."

Gillian stepped away, shaken. Will gave her a look that said he wished there could be a lot more where that came from before escorting her off the dance floor. All she wanted to do was drag Will to the parking lot or somewhere they could talk about what just happened, but Tasha was in the mood to celebrate. Gillian had barely recovered from the shaky feeling in her legs when Tasha and several of their friends swept her back toward the dance floor. Gillian reached a hand out to Will.

"You coming?"

He laughed. "No. I'd sooner eat barbed wire than line dance."

She laughed, surprised there was anything at all he wouldn't do. She personally loved line dancing. It was great exercise, and the songs were always fun. Every now and then she'd smile back at him from the dance floor, showing off her moves. He stood there smiling back with his thumbs hooked in his jeans pockets, and she wondered how they were going to define their relationship now.

"What was happening to you two out here?" Tasha was huffing beside her as they did an intricate move with their feet.

"I think that was obvious," Gillian answered, no

longer trying to deny it.

Tasha smiled. "You two *are* hot for each other."

"We aren't in high school."

"No, but I bet you wish you were. Then you wouldn't have to worry about that agent-manager thing."

"We were caught up in the moment."

"A very hot moment," Tasha pointed out. Before Gillian could answer, she tried the next step. Failing, the two crashed into each other, exploding into giggles. They walked off the floor together.

Will stood off to the side, hat now on his head. He was a sight to behold, and a glance around reminded her that she wasn't the only one to notice.

"I think I'll get home," he said. "I've a lot of work to do."

"You work too hard." Gillian gave him a light punch in the arm before boldly sidling up close to him.

He slid one arm around her waist, yanked her closer, and gazed down at her. "Probably not as hard as you've been working."

"Thank you for noticing."

He shook his head. "I've never seen a musician who works harder. I'm only sorry to say you're about to be even busier."

"Then I better party while I can." She was conscious of how his hand pressed against her lower back, locking her securely against his body. She stared up at him under the shadow of his hat.

"Why don't you stay and have some more fun?" she said. "It's been forever since I've been in a place like this without an apron and a tray of drinks."

She recognized the desire in his eyes because it mirrored her own as he leaned close to say something in her ear. She tilted her head, shivering as his lips brushed her cheek.

"I believe if I don't leave now, I might say or do

something we'll both regret later."

Emboldened by his frank admission, she turned to whisper in his ear.

She let her lips graze the sideburns of his temple and whispered, "How do you know I'll regret it?"

He caught her around the waist with both hands, pressing her firmly, but tenderly, against him. He smiled.

"Woman, you don't know what you're saying. We barely know each other. You're just caught up in all this excitement. Have you had anything to drink?" His eyes traveled around the room and landed back on her.

"No, I haven't, and how do you know what I'm caught up in? I know who I am and am not attracted to."

His grin widened. His eyes slipped down to her lips and back up to gaze hungrily into hers. "OK, I do know what you're caught up in tonight, but you need to focus on that guitar. And I'm going to let you, no matter how crazy just being around you makes me."

"Maybe it's you who makes me crazy," she countered, her chest rising and falling from the breathless feel of being so close.

Backing slightly away, his eyes now traveled appreciatively over her. He let out a sigh, shaking his head back and forth.

"Where this is leading is a bad idea, Gillian. Trust me on this." His hand trailed lower on her hip and he squeezed. "Or rather, don't trust me, darlin'."

He gave her a rueful smile. She gulped a breath.

"You're the boss," she said, gently backing away.

"No," he said. "I'm working for you."

"Then do what I say," she teased, trying not to beg. "Stay."

"But you see?" He leaned over her again and whispered, his voice low and hot against her ear. "I don't want to stay here with you."

Her heart fell.

"I want to take you home."

Her pulse rushed to her head, and she felt woozy with the extremes of emotion sweeping through her body. He gave her a wicked smile and straightened up to his full height. She was torn, wanting to take him up on his offer, and yet the last thing her heart wanted was some tryst with Will—she wanted much more than that.

She opened her mouth to say something, but he held up a hand.

"Shh. It wasn't an invitation, darlin'. I don't want you to be a one-night stand." He turned and walked away, leaving her heart pounding and raw.

That was it, then—the end of a tryst that never even happened. She tried to convince herself she didn't want it anyway, and a commitment at this stage in her career would break her own rule, never mind Will's professional standards. And Will wasn't even the commitment type, manager or not. She didn't know why she'd ever entertained the idea in the first place. And yet, as she watched him walk away, she did know.

Casting a look at her friends, she saw Tasha duck her head. Gillian hoped she didn't look as dejected as she felt, but that's what she got for forgetting her own rules. She watched the back of Will's cowboy hat swimming away across the sea of people and resolved to forget about this by tomorrow. They'd let their obvious attraction to each other get in the way, but tomorrow it was back to agent and client. Gathering up her feelings, she was turning to join her friends when she saw Will's cowboy hat change direction.

He was walking back to her, with purpose, his eyes determined as he reached for her. His feelings must not have been cooperating with his intelligence any more than hers when he nuzzled into the cascade of her hair and she felt his warm lips pressing the soft skin of her neck, and briefly on her lips, the warmth making her long for something deeper, before he tore himself away and left, leaving her head spinning.

She grasped the rail separating the dining area from the dance floor and tried to force away the thoughts that made her want to rush and catch up with him.

"That didn't help," she whispered.

Her momma used to tell her not to give up her music dreams for boys, but she hadn't warned her that once the boys grew up, they might be impossible to resist.

ॐ

Will slammed the door of his pickup truck.

"Idiot."

He rested his hands on the steering wheel with a heavy sigh, letting the rumbling truck idle for a minute before he would hit the interstate and head off to his huge empty mansion in Brentwood. At the rate he was going, it would continue to be empty too. He'd known plenty of women, but he never offered them Brentwood. Not even the woman he'd been serious with a few years back, choosing to instead live with her in a luxury Nashville apartment.

Gillian, on the other hand, was different. For some inexplicable reason, he wanted to show his home in Brentwood to her. It was idiotic, perhaps, but he wanted to show her the barn where he planned to have horses someday, the bedrooms his mom decorated for him and the big kitchen where he secretly envisioned kids eating breakfast before school. These thoughts had been running through his head since he met her, and it wasn't appropriate—he was trying to get her a record deal, not turn her into a housewife. And yet, she was so beautiful, so alluring, and she didn't even know it. He knew he was playing with fire, but he could barely keep his mind—or his hands—off her.

It could only end in heartbreak. Even without their business relationship, they were too different. He was what his sisters called wild. Always had been. The only women he dated were older than Gillian and wanted exactly what he wanted: no strings. Gillian, on the other hand—he shook his head in the cab of his truck—was a good woman. She had an innocence about her that made him feel protective, but still an unexpected ability to flirt—and a body—that made him want to sleep with her and wonder what their babies would look like. The last part scared the hell out of him. In fact, she was the kind of woman he'd grown up in his own small town thinking he'd end up with someday after all his carousing was over.

Flipping the AC on, he waited for the gush of cold air, but nothing could cool the emotions burning through him. A buzz in his pocket interrupted his thoughts, and he pulled out his cell. A text from Gillian. His heart gave a little lurch that made him feel like a teenage boy.

"Come back," she'd written, followed by a smiley face emoji. He chuckled. Even she wanted to play with fire, and it made him want to show her how he was starting to feel.

Hell—not starting to feel. It'd already happened. From the moment he saw her wobbling around in those crazy shoes in his lobby, he'd fallen for her. He reached for the gear shift, knowing he needed to get her out of his system, and the memory of her hips against him sent his mind reeling.

He paused. The heck with it all. Maybe he should go back inside, get to her apartment and see what happened—see if they could get it out of their systems and move on.

Then he slapped the wheel. No way.

He didn't think he could face himself the next day if he used Gillian Heart. Her dreams were on the line, and she was too inexperienced to realize it. And if by some twist of fate it ended up being more than a fling, would she blame him if he couldn't get her a deal? What would she do then? He didn't think she'd have a problem getting a new agent, but one never really knew in this business.

"Why me?" The memory of her eyes right after he kissed her seared through him. She'd looked so vulnerable, so beautiful, he'd barely been able to tear his eyes off her long enough to leave The Spur.

He reluctantly texted her back. "Wish I could. Gotta get home."

"Damn it all." He jammed the truck in gear and drove toward Brentwood, driving fast enough to get a ticket. He knew what he needed to do.

# Chapter Nine

"He did?" Gillian tried not to look hurt, but she felt smacked in the jaw.

"Will changed your schedule," Josie said apologetically. "You're now with Dorothy."

"But Dorothy's not my manager." Gillian lowered her voice. "What's going on?"

"He's still your agent," Josie said, placing a reassuring hand on her arm. "He just put Dorothy in charge of your day-to-day management."

Gillian shook her head. "Why?"

Josie shrugged.

"But I don't even know Dorothy."

Josie smiled. "Don't worry. You're gonna be in good hands, honey. Dorothy has a ton of experience in this town."

Will's office door swung open before she could work out what to do. She could see he was all business with his arms crossed impatiently across his chest, as if he hadn't wrapped those same arms around her last night in The

Steel Spur. Behind him stood a pretty black woman who appeared to be in her thirties.

She smiled at the woman who must be Dorothy, then cast her attention on Will.

"You don't want to manage me any more?" She hoped she didn't sound whiny, but she felt like crying. Will was the only one besides Tasha and her momma who really knew about her hopes and dreams. She'd shared some of her deepest feelings, even the real story behind her dad, with Will. It'd been an act of trust to open up about some of those things, and she couldn't imagine establishing that relationship with someone else. Plus, when would they be able to spend any time together now?

He looked at her, his face unreadable. "I take it Josie explained it to you."

Then she realized he must not want to spend time with her. He'd made it clear last night he didn't want a one-night stand, and he was a one-night stand kind of guy. How else did he ooze sexual charm the way he did? Her chest tightened as the truth sank in. She was a fool.

"No, I did not," Josie said. "I just broke the news. You'll need to explain it to her yourself." She sat down and turned to her computer screen.

Will sighed and crooked his finger at Gillian. She followed him and Dorothy into his office.

"I know what this is about." Gillian looked at Will.

"You might think you do, but you don't," he said softly. "The main point, Gillian, is that I don't have time to add you to my daily schedule."

"I'm sorry," she said, thinking of all the time they'd been spending together. Somehow she knew it wasn't normal to hang out with your music manager that often, but she'd told herself it was because she was a new client and he was trying to show her the ropes. It must have been the attraction that made him spend all that time with her, and now they were getting back to business.

He smiled. "Don't be sorry, darlin'."

Dorothy chose that moment to stick her hand out. Gillian shook it. She had nothing against Dorothy, now having remembered seeing her in the office once before, but they'd never even been introduced. Now she was in charge of Gillian's career? Gillian took a calming breath, wanting to give Dorothy a chance but frustrated at Will.

Dorothy cleared her throat. "I'm one of Will's day-to-day managers, which is exactly what it sounds like. Will brokers all the deals, but he can't handle all the clients. I take some of them and handle all those daily things like accepting calls about you, scheduling appointments and interviews, going with you to events, recordings and television appearances. That kind of thing."

Things like The Steel Spur, Gillian thought. And she bet Dorothy didn't dance with her clients either. In that regard, working with her could be simpler.

"Like a publicist?" Gillian asked.

Dorothy nodded. "I'm a little bit of that too. Now, I know Will has a busy day ahead, so if you will, let's move this meeting over to my office." She walked out, leaving Gillian alone with Will.

"She'll just be a minute," Will told Dorothy before closing the door to his office.

"What are you thinking?" he asked. "You look upset."

"Why are you giving me up?"

"Darlin', I could never give you up. I'm trying to give you a career."

"By handing me off to a lower manager?"

"First of all. Dorothy wouldn't like hearing you describe her as a lower manager. She's got an important job, and trust me, she's on her way up. She could run this company without me."

Chastened, Gillian nodded. "OK, I'm sorry. I get that, but this just isn't at all what I was expecting."

"You think it's normal for a manager to spend all his time with one client?"

"No," she said.

He gave her a crooked smile. "So, what do you think my other clients think about you hogging all my time? What kind of client does that?"

She was taken aback for a second, not knowing if he was teasing or serious.

"I guess the kind of client you kissed and danced with and wanted to take home."

He nodded. "Now we're getting somewhere."

She leaned against his desk, turning what he'd said over in her mind.

"What are you going to do while I'm being managed by Dorothy?"

"Besides paying some attention to my other clients, several who are getting jealous, I'll have more time to negotiate the big things for you. The things that'll make you a star, unless that's not what you hired me to do." His jaw twitched.

She knew Will worked for her, but since she had no cards to hold, the concept seemed ludicrous.

"I was caught off guard," she said. "I guess I'm all right with it."

"That's my girl."

His girl. She wished. Then a thought flitted through her mind.

What if?

The memory of him, so close to her on the darkened dance floor, his hands on her hips, the pulse of his neck, made her want to say how she really felt. She wished she knew what he was thinking right now, but he was silent. To keep from looking at him, she studied the awards, the photographs, the small trophy sitting in a glass case.

"Wait. You won a Grammy?" She wondered how she'd missed it during their first meeting? It must have been nerves.

The corners of his mouth tugged upward, but he didn't smile.

"How come you never told me?" She crossed the room to study it closer. "Will. This is amazing!"

"No big deal. It's for songwriting, way back when I first came to Nashville."

"You didn't tell me about it."

"It was a long time ago. I was barely out of high school."

"Hey, wait a minute." She leaned closer, studied the trophy, not believing what she was seeing, but there it was, etched into a Grammy. Her dad's name. She slowly turned to Will, who gave her a guarded look.

"Why wouldn't you have told me that?" Her voice was barely a whisper.

He shrugged. "It didn't seem to matter."

A heaviness gathered like rocks in her belly.

"I wish you'd told me as soon as you knew he was my dad."

"Would it have made a difference in your signing with me?"

She honestly didn't know, but it made her stop and think a minute now. "You wrote songs with Cooper Heart, and the two of you shared a Grammy?" She felt like she was being rammed in the side by a two-by-four.

He stood, took a few tentative steps in her direction. "I'm sorry."

"It's just a shock," she said. "One more thing my dad shut me out of." She wondered why her momma hadn't told her. Moisture was building in the corners of her eyes like a bucket on a water wheel about to reach the top of its rotation.

"How did you end up working with him?" She kept

her eyes glued on the trophy.

"I was only a kid," he said. "Sometimes your dad participated in a roundtable of songwriters who—"

"I know. He came here every month to work. He used to take me with him, but when I was about eleven or so, he started leaving me at home."

Will nodded. "I wouldn't have wanted to work with him if I'd known what a poor father he was—"

"Oh, he wasn't poor." She added her own meaning to the word and angrily swiped her eyes. "He was rich."

"That was probably true."

"But you wouldn't have known if you'd seen that his only daughter lived in a single-wide, run-down trailer with her mom who had to work two and three jobs at a time to pay the bills. I even had to help out. Did you know that? I come by my waitressing skills honestly."

Will's eyes filled with compassion. "Hell, I didn't know it was that bad for you."

She sniffed and crossed her arms at her chest. "We didn't need a fancy house or anything like that, but a phone call would've been nice."

She plopped down in a chair beside the trophy case and gazed resentfully at the award.

"I guess my dad has one of these trophies too, right?"

Will nodded.

"I didn't even know he won a Grammy," she said, her voice cracking, and in that moment she realized how utterly banned she and her mom had been from her dad's life.

She pressed her hands against her eyes.

"How often do you talk to my dad anyway?" she asked through her hands. "Have you told him about me?"

❧

Will gazed at the trophy that'd always made him so proud. The trophy was one of the things he could usually point out to a potential client who was on the fence, and he'd win them over just like that. Now he felt almost ashamed of it. He'd looked up to Cooper Heart back then, grateful for the step up. He'd had no idea about Cooper's family—no idea about Gillian.

Now he knew about his daughter. Hell, he was in love with her, and it killed him to see her staring at the trophy case, her face a mixture of fury and sadness.

"I probably hear from your dad a few times a year," he said, honestly. This admission made her flinch, but he was afraid to touch her. She looked like she might shatter.

"When is the last time you talked to him?"

He walked to his desk and consulted his calendar. "Three months ago."

She looked up, her wide red eyes moist, but her cheeks dry. "Really?"

He nodded.

"He hasn't called me in ten years, at least."

"He's obviously not who I thought he was," Will said.

"At least not to my mom and me."

He sighed. "But listen, sweetheart. Maybe you two can patch things up, write some songs together, maybe—" The look in her eyes stopped him mid-sentence.

"Please don't ever say that again." She sniffed.

"People in music are going to find out," he said.

"I don't care. I've disowned him."

He turned away, wishing she'd change her mind. She'd be ticked, but he'd already had to play the Cooper Heart card with one of the biggest labels around, and as a result, they wanted to listen to her demo. He would've been crazy not to do it.

When he turned back, his eyes fell on her sagging

form. Oh, good Lord. What kind of father could leave his little girl?

She was burying her face in her hands, her small shoulders quaking. It filled him with remorse, and damn it, with a feeling that was more than mere attraction. He wanted to shelter her, to guard her heart, to make her feel safe. He wanted to take her home, and not just to make love to her, but to make her part of his world. He wanted all of her. Will's heart pounded with each realization that he'd already fallen hard for his newest, most inexperienced and most promising client. The situation was like a dynamite stick waiting to ignite.

With two strides he walked to his office door and lowered the shades. Dorothy could wait. He strode back to Gillian. Gently taking her by the shoulders, he lifted her to her feet. Her hands were still pressed over her face.

He gripped her shoulders, his heart ripping with every sorrowful shake.

"I'm so sorry, darlin'. I should've put that stupid trophy away."

Her face was still buried in her hands and damp strands of hair were plastered to her cheeks. Tissues. She probably needed a whole box. He let go of her long enough to search his office, opening and closing drawers until he found them.

"Darlin'. You're killing me."

She sniffed, choking on a remarkable amount of snot. It made him laugh in spite of himself.

"I'm a mess."

He handed her the box of tissues.

"You're definitely not a mess. Unless it's a hot mess you're talking about."

"That's a really bad come-on line." She pulled herself up straight and attempted a smile. "Does it usually work?"

She was gorgeous staring at him through glistening eyes. Desire welled up in him. He moved closer.

"I don't know. I usually try not to make women cry."

Not caring that they were in his office, he cupped her cheeks in his hands, running his thumbs gently along the damp skin under her eyes. She didn't move, except for her body still quivering from emotion. He wanted to kiss away every tear, every bit of pain and fear. He hadn't ever cared about someone like he did Gillian, and if he could just take her home and treat her special like she deserved, he'd know what to do, but there in his office he was at a loss for how to help.

"It looks like we've barely gotten started, and I've already hurt you."

"My dad is not your fault," she said. "I'm still happy about your Grammy. I only wish my own dad had told me about it."

She took a breath, closed her eyes. Her lips, damp from tears and pink from her self-consciously biting them for the past ten minutes, were full and irresistible. Eyes wide open, he leaned forward and brushed his lips on hers, light as a feather at first. He watched her face, and when she didn't flinch away, he kissed the salt off them, gently, and the taste of her made him want to kiss her full on the mouth. But he was patient, testing the waters first to see if last night at The Steel Spur had been a fluke.

He kissed a tear-smudged eyelid. "Listen. You can work with me instead of Dorothy if you want to, but I can't get any work done that way." He kissed the other eyelid. "Because every minute I'm with you, I want to do this." A soft moan escaped her lips as he gently parted them with his own, and that was all the permission he needed to kiss her the way he wanted. Yearning jolted through him as the pressure of her lips progressed from gentle to maddening.

She kissed him back with a fever he hadn't expected, and when he felt her hands slide up his back, he wished they weren't trapped in his office. Somewhere in the background he heard his phone ringing, but he ignored it.

"Will," she whispered, gasping for breath. He forced himself to let go, afraid she'd changed her mind about what she wanted. Her eyes still sparkled with tears, making him want to kiss her all over again.

He drew in a shaky breath. "What's wrong? You don't want this?" Disappointment
settled like a brick in the center of his chest. He took a small step back.

"Yes I do, it's just that—" She grabbed the front of his shirt and pulled him to her. A jolt of excitement plunged through him. Obviously whatever she wanted to say could wait a little longer. She kissed him with a passion he'd only fantasized about when he thought of her in his big empty house at night, and he responded by pulling her tight against him. When he felt her body meld to his, he broke from her kiss only long enough to press his lips against her neck, loving how it made her gasp.

A loud rap at the door brought them back to reality.

"Damn it." He let her go, walked to the door and cracked it open. "What is it, Josie?"

"Dorothy wants to know if you'll be letting her see Gillian Heart any time today."

Will turned back to Gillian who was still catching her breath. He raised his eyebrows in question. She nodded, attempting to smooth her disheveled appearance. Thank heavens, because he definitely couldn't be subjected to these kinds of office meetings every day and expect to not go crazy from wanting to kiss her.

"She'll be there in a few minutes." He shut the door and walked back to Gillian. He grasped her hands, held them tight.

"Listen, darlin'. I've been pulling my teeth out trying to figure how we can see each other and it not be as complicated for us as agent and client. That's the real reason I put you with Dorothy."

She was silent for a few seconds. "So does this mean we get to go out on a date now?"

"I sure hope so."

"Wow, a real date. No more fake coffee meetings."

"You figured out they were fake?"

"It'd crossed my mind. But now if we go on a real date, what will we ever talk about?"

He squeezed her hand. "You mean we have to talk?"

That'd just slipped out. She playfully punched him in the arm. A rap on the door made them both jump.

"Dorothy awaits." He promised himself he'd explain about his telling the record executives about her dad later.

She raised herself up on the toes of her boots to kiss him briefly on the mouth. He caught her by the waist, and an ache that started in the center of his chest spread through the rest of his body. Before he could stop himself, he was kissing her again.

# Chapter Ten

A few weeks later, they were sitting on a secluded bench in Centennial Park and had been making out like two teenagers. They'd spent the afternoon at The Parthenon, a Nashville landmark Gillian had never visited before, then meandered through the park. The Tennessee heat had ebbed away, and a light breeze was flowing, giving Gillian a nostalgic feeling of home. It was nice to have no schedule for the weekend, something that hadn't happened since she moved there.

She leaned over and wrapped her arms around Will's neck. "Kiss me again."

His lips were warm and urgent on hers. Emboldened by the knowledge that he felt the same for her as she did for him, she let her lips trail from his, to his slightly stubbled jaw, and finally the warm skin of his neck, causing him to emit a low moan. He caught her by the chin.

"Gillian Heart, you make me want to behave like a rogue."

A thrill leapt through her, giving her the same feeling she'd always felt on the Ferris wheel during the Fourth of July celebration in Gold Creek Gap.

"You aren't a rogue." She traced a hand up one lean, muscular arm. "But we are two grown individuals in a public park."

"At sunset," he said. "That's when I turn into a rogue." He pulled her against him, his hands on her waist softly nudging away the barriers she'd erected to protect herself from men like Robert who use women, who leave their hearts bruised, and who leave, period.

"Mmm," she moaned. He nuzzled her neck, and shivers spread through her body.

"You know," he whispered, his voice gruff with heat. "We could take this back to your apartment."

Her heart was like a hummingbird caught in a cage. He probably wondered why this hadn't happened already, but while her body was willing, her brain still wasn't. What was she supposed to tell him? Um, sorry, I can't have sex with you unless it's for forever, as in I would prefer to be your wife first, since the last man I had a relationship with used my body and broke my heart. She ran a hand up his arm, enjoying the way he was built, because as protective as she was about her heart, she wasn't immune to his charm or his physique.

He kissed the skin below her ear, causing a shiver at the back of her neck.

"What do you say, darlin'?"

She pulled back, her mind clouded with a smoldering desire that was too easily smothered by memories of being hurt. Will's reputation for trifling with women didn't help at all in the trust department, either. She didn't even want to think about how many times he must have taken a woman home. She, on the other hand, was a small-town, simple girl whose few experiences in relationships hadn't taught her much about love, except that it ended in broken hearts. Running her hand affectionately along his arm, she teasingly squeezed his bicep and tried to change the subject.

"You are very fit," she said. "Especially for someone who happens to be a card-carrying workaholic."

"It's from all the running. That's why I'm so skinny." He made a big show of flexing his guns. "Sorry I'm not a buff body builder. Is that your type?"

"No." She laughed at his antics. "But I wonder, do you run in boots or something?"

"You think I live in cowboy boots?"

"No, but you would if you could."

He laughed, reminding her how she loved the way his eyes crinkled at the corners when he smiled. "I do mostly live in boots, but I take them off when I need to." She didn't miss the implication behind his words. He tipped her chin up, taking her face in his hands. His lips were gentle, tender, slow—tantalizingly slow. A sigh slipped from her as quiet as the rustle of breeze in the trees of the park.

"Take me home," she said. In the fading light, his eyes brightened. "Just for a drink," she added coyly.

"We'll see about that," he said, pulling her to her feet and leading her toward his truck.

❧

Inside her apartment, she ran around picking up stray clothing and Tasha's coffee cups, which Tasha had a way of leaving all over the place. She gathered a pile of magazines to move them out of the way.

"I'm sorry," she said. "I need to clean this place up."

"If you'd move in with me, you wouldn't have to. I have a housekeeper."

She froze in place, waiting for her heart to start beating again.

"What?"

"Move in with me," he said.

Her face flooded with heat.

She cleared her throat. "Why would you want me to do that? Are you wanting to help me out or something? Because Tasha and I are doing fine here." She gestured around her tiny apartment.

"Sure. I'd like to help you out." He grinned. "I have a list of things I could help you with, if you moved in with me."

"I'm sure you do," she said, enjoying his little game. "How much would rent be?"

"No rent."

She grinned. "Are you serious, or is that another come-on line?"

His expression grew thoughtful. "It's actually not a come-on line, unless you want it to be."

He took the magazines she held and tossed them to the coffee table. Her heartbeat quickened when they slid sideways to reveal several bridal titles. Reading bride magazines was one of the things she and Tasha did to unwind after work while they watched romantic movies, flipping through the magazines like two teenage girls and planning their weddings. They each had a Pinterest board for the same purpose, and a few days ago Tasha had played a joke on her by pinning a picture of Will Adams in a cowboy hat on Gillian's wedding board. Thank goodness Will wasn't the pin board type.

She noted the smile on his face and wondered if he was serious about the moving in or just teasing her. They didn't know each other well enough to be moving in together.

"When does Tasha get home?" he asked.

"She's in Memphis visiting her family."

"So you're all alone?" He grinned like a Cheshire cat.

"Yes. A drink?"

"Definitely."

She grabbed a Coke and a beer. They toasted the fact that they'd found each other as they leaned against the counter side by side.

"I'm serious about you moving in," he said. Setting his beer down, he moved closer and wrapped an arm around her shoulders. "I want to spend a heck of a lot more time with you and not just when we're working."

The idea of moving in with him sent a thrill right through her, and then it soured in her stomach. Someone else had asked her to move in once, and it had ended badly.

"We're not working now," she said.

"That's a good point," he said. "Which means we should be talking less and doing more of this." He pressed his lips softly against hers, teasing, and then he leaned lower to trail kiss after kiss along her neck, causing little shivers to dance across her skin. A sigh escaped her lips, and she leaned her head just so, letting him know he could keep doing that. Before she realized it, so swept away with her desire to be touched by him, he'd picked her up and set her on the countertop in front of him. She gasped when he inched her shirt up, sending a surge of heat through her body.

Will whispered between kisses. "You know I'm serious, don't you? Move in with me. We could be alone like this all the time."

"Hmm. Tempting." He had no idea.

"How tempting?"

"More than you know," she said, breathless.

He pulled back to look at her. "The idea of living together makes you nervous."

She kissed him on the cheek. "It's not my style to move in with someone because we're dating. Been there and done that. It turned out badly."

Letting go, he leaned back on the counter beside her

and took a long drink. She tried to read how disappointed he was about her response, but if she was going to date someone like Will, she needed to let him know her standards. She needed to know what he thought of them. She wasn't going to be in a situation like the last one, where she had given up everything to a man, and got nothing but pain and sorrow in return. No wonder there were so many country songs about cheating and broken hearts. They were based on truth.

"I'm curious," he said. "How many boyfriends have you had?"

She blinked. "A few. One was my senior year in high school, if that counts. We broke up after graduation."

"Poor guy," he said.

"Such are the lessons of young love."

"What lesson did *you* learn?"

"Boys just wanted to mess around," she said. "They didn't understand that I had responsibilities other girls didn't have. And besides, boys were a distraction from my dreams."

"So you've had two serious boyfriends? Your high school love? And then the one you moved in with?"

"During my first year in Nashville."

He was silent for a while. "He hurt you?"

"It's not a big deal," she said.

"Is that why you're so reluctant to give in and let yourself fall for me?"

She laughed. "Trust me. I've fallen for you."

He nudged her with his elbow. "But you're holding back."

She gave a sad sigh. "I'm just being careful."

He laced his hand through hers. "How long are you going to keep being careful?"

She wanted to say, not long, but the thought of taking another risk like the one she'd taken before both excited and terrified her.

"Before you, you know, I'd given up on men altogether, at least while pursuing my music dreams. So being with you now is me giving men another chance."

"Most women don't give up on men until they've been divorced a couple of times."

"Most women don't also have a dad who—" Her voice cracked, and she chugged her Coke. She couldn't finish her sentence. They'd known each other just long enough that she hoped she didn't need to.

He squeezed her knee. "Dads can really screw things up for little girls, can't they?"

She shrugged. "Not all dads. You have sisters. Did your dad treat them well?"

"He was a saint with them," he said, his eyes staring at the dark window behind her. "They are, all but one, married now with kids of their own, none the worse for wear. Happy."

She felt wistful. "Lucky girls."

"Listen," he said. "Just because your dad didn't do his job, doesn't mean your mom didn't do a damned good job in his place."

She raised her drink in the air. "To moms."

"They're special, and so are you," he said, his eyes serious. "Someday, you'll be like my sisters, with a litter of kids running around at your heels, and you'll be a great mom and have a great career at the same time."

She decided not to chastise him about referring to kids as a litter, and instead let her thoughts wander, imagining what kind of father he'd be. He didn't seem like the kind of man who wanted to settle down, even if he had just asked her to move in.

"Was your dad good to you?" she asked.

"I didn't think so at the time. It's hard being a preacher's kid. He was hell-bent on making a man out of me, but it took a long time. I wasn't an easy kid."

She laughed. "I bet my momma wouldn't have let me

go out with you."

"I bet my dad wouldn't have let me go out with you, to save your momma the worry, but I would have anyway. And the two of us together would've been trouble."

She smiled wider, thinking about what he'd have gotten her into if his charm in high school was anything like it was now.

"You turned out to be a good man," she said.

"I think the jury's still out on that." He swung his gaze back to her, his eyebrows crinkling. "So, I take it you moved in with this man you dated when you first moved to Nashville?"

"For one week, and then on the seventh day, I came home to find him in a very compromising position with a girl from the diner. Thank the good Lord Tasha hadn't found another roommate to replace me yet." She hopped down from the counter. Realizing she needed something stronger, she grabbed the opened bottle of chardonnay from the fridge and poured herself a glass.

"Holy smokes," he said, gently.

She took a sip and looked up at him, a sad smile on her face. "Before I moved in, he gave me a ring."

He set his beer down. "Oh, darlin'."

"It's crazy, right? Ask a girl to marry you, and then cheat on her as soon as she moves in?"

"Yeah," he said, nodding his head. "But what's worse is if the girl he hurt never moves on."

She shot him a dirty look.

He held his hands up, palms out. "Now don't look at me like that. You want to know what I really think?"

"I'm not sure, but you're about to tell me."

"I think that other guy is an idiot, and that thanks to him, you are being too careful."

"And you think you're the kind of guy I don't need to be careful around? You've admitted yourself that you don't have the best track record." She smiled to soften the blow, but if she was going to date him, she wanted to be honest. His way with women made her nervous.

He had the decency to look chastened. "I haven't always been a good man."

Feeling guilty, she gave him an apologetic look. "Well, you are now, but I've been on the other side of that. My heart's warning me to slow down. I don't want to move in, or do anything else, until I know you're in it for keeps."

He crossed his arms, stared at her. Finally, he nodded. "So, does that mean I do or I don't get to see you naked tonight?"

She laughed out loud, unable to keep her serious face on for one more minute.

"You are such a big flirt. And the answer is no."

He looked disappointed, but his eyes still twinkled. "I think you need to be more spontaneous."

"I can be spontaneous," she said.

"Sure. When's the last time you ripped off your clothes and ran around naked just for fun?"

"With my friend Tommy."

His face darkened. "Who's Tommy?"

"He's my neighbor back in Gold Creek Gap, and we went skinny dipping in the sprinkler when we were three."

He smiled broadly. "I have a sprinkler."

"You are shameless," she said, unable to keep from laughing. Maybe this would all work out. She didn't know what was going to happen with her and Will, but considering he hadn't run off as soon as she turned him down, she had a feeling it might be good.

When he finally left a few hours later, after letting her subject him to two Hallmark movies, he kissed her lightly at the door.

"I'm surprised you aren't still trying to stay the

night," she said matter-of-factly, not sure if she wanted him to ask again or if she wanted him to leave. Her head, heart and body were definitely in conflict either way.

"Not tonight, darlin'. You aren't ready." He pulled her close. "I will get you to trust me someday, though. Watch out."

"Consider me warned," she said.

He grunted. "Just keep in mind, I have a big empty house with enough beds to host half your hometown for a weekend. You can't blame me for wanting company."

"I didn't say I wouldn't visit."

"Good." He moved to leave. "Lock your door, OK?"

"OK." She always did, but it was sweet of him to worry about her well-being.

"This isn't the safest part of town," he said. "You know, at least if you won't move to Brentwood with me, I'd be happy to help you girls find something else."

"And pay the company back when I earn song royalties?" It was something she'd heard Dorothy and Josie say lots in the past few weeks as she purchased new clothes for photo shoots, interviews and performances.

"The company wouldn't be paying," he said. "I would."

She gazed at him, amazed at his generous heart, but she couldn't take advantage.

"I'd never accept that kind of help from you, but thanks." She placed her hand affectionately against his chest. "You don't think you're good inside, Will. But you are."

"Then I'm trustworthy, right?" He winked.

She scoffed. "I'm sorry. I don't mean to be that kind of girl who sends a guy mixed signals."

He placed a finger over her lips. "Don't apologize. I don't know what's going to happen to us. I've hurt every woman I've ever been serious with, but I promise, I won't hurt you. I love you."

She blinked hard. "You do?"

His eyes grew serious. "Yeah. And it scares the crap out of me."

She touched his face. "But how can you know already?" She laughed softly. "Are you teasing?"

He smiled. "No joking right now, Gillian Heart."

"It's nutty, but... I love you too." She was breathless with the saying and the knowing of it. "But it's too soon."

He caught her chin in his hand. "I fell for you when I saw you in that little tease of an outfit in my lobby, and then again at The Blue Fiddle in those hot little jeans and boots of yours singing that Patsy Cline song."

"You mean *Crazy*. And I was wearing more than hot little jeans and boots."

"You were?" He pulled her close, running one hand softly up her spine and back down to her waist where he fiddled with her belt loops. "I don't remember that. I must've been looking right through the rest."

His hands burned through the thin fabric of her blouse. He kissed her long and sweet.

With a low groan, his hands moved to cup her face.

"Why do you have to be *that* kind of girl?" But he smiled his crooked grin when he said it.

"Sorry." It was on the tip of her tongue to say she'd move in with him after all, but she remembered another piece of her momma's advice. Make him work for it. If he doesn't mind going a few extra miles, he means it.

"Don't be," he said. "It's sweet that you're old-fashioned."

"Me, old-fashioned? After all that kissing, how can you say that?"

※※

Will kissed her firmly, trailing one hand along her

thigh and the other over the curve of her hip. He wanted so much more than kissing. Heat rushed over him in waves, and he pulled her into a tight embrace so he'd keep his hands off her. Lord have mercy.

"How can I say you're old-fashioned? Because it's a lot of just kissing, darlin'."

She placed her hand on his chest. Her eyes were clouded with desire but troubled too.

He groaned. "Don't worry. It's sexy."

And with a shock that exploded through his mind, he realized it was more than sexy. It made him want her more than ever, more than any woman he'd ever had— and not just in his bed.

## Chapter Eleven

"Are you nervous?" Dorothy asked.

They were in Dorothy's car headed to meet Will at a big record label meeting. Will had told her to be ready, that they were right on the edge of signing her to a deal, but it hadn't seemed possible. She couldn't believe it. It hadn't even been that long since she'd signed a contract to be represented by Adams Music, and now she was about to meet with industry executives. She popped the visor down and fussed with her hair and lipstick again, wishing she could smooth her nerves out the way she could her hair.

"You look fine," Dorothy said.

"I feel like I'm going to throw up."

"Don't do that. My husband will have a cow if you mess up this car."

Gillian laughed to think of Dorothy worrying about upsetting her husband. She was so tough; it was hard to even imagine her being a wife.

"How long have you been married?" Gillian asked,

hoping to distract herself from the fact that her stomach felt like it was in her throat.

"Ten years this past weekend, as a matter of fact."

"Wow. Congratulations." Gillian tried to imagine being married for so long.

"Kids?"

"Two boys," she said, her voice filled with pride. "Five and seven."

"Wow, Dorothy. You're amazing. How do you handle being a mom and having such a great career at the same time?" Gillian hoped she didn't sound as wistful as she felt.

"I'm not doing it alone," she said. "I'm doing it with their dad. And I do it because I love it, both my kids and my career, but my kids and husband win out every time."

"I want that too," Gillian confided. "But I want to have my career first, then see about the rest." She didn't mention how Will had made her start to rethink some of that plan.

"That's not a bad strategy," Dorothy said. "Even though sometimes the heart has its own agenda."

Gillian sighed. "Dorothy, do you think I'm making a mistake by seeing Will outside of work?"

"I'd be lying if I said it didn't worry me. Just be careful. Women have a hard enough time being taken seriously in this business already."

Gillian knew Dorothy was right. Her momma had said the same thing a hundred times.

"I hope you don't think I'm dating him to get ahead of the other clients." That was the last thing Gillian wanted to be known for, especially by Dorothy.

"I think you two are smitten," Dorothy said. "And who knows? Maybe the two of you'll get married and be as beloved in the industry as Faith and Tim. But trust me. As one of the few black women working in country music, I know something about how hard it is to earn respect in this industry. Being a woman in this biz isn't easy, period, even without huge obstacles. Don't put hurdles in your own way, OK?"

Gillian wanted to dismiss Dorothy's advice, pretend there was nothing atypical about dating your music manager when you were a brand new client, but she'd been in Nashville long enough to know she was playing with fire. And it wasn't like Gillian to do that.

"Are you saying I shouldn't see him?"

"Who am I to stop love?" Dorothy asked. "It's obvious you two are hotter than a pepper sprout, just like that old song says, so not seeing him is probably not an option. Go ahead and get it out of your system, but just trust me. Keep your personal and business lives apart as much as you can. That, of course, is part of the reason Will gave you to me, but I'm invested in you, Gillian. I'm not going to steer you wrong."

"OK." Gillian appreciated Dorothy's honesty. It was better than tiptoeing around the issue. "And thank you."

"Just remember he's your agent at this meeting," Dorothy said. "Nothing else."

"So." Gillian couldn't hide a grin. "No kissing him or holding hands while he's making deals."

Dorothy chuckled. "Exactly, honey. As far as the record company is concerned, you and Will aren't lovers. You aren't even friends. It's best not to advertise who you're sleeping with in this business, whether he's your agent or not."

Gillian felt her face flush. "Actually, we haven't gone there yet."

Dorothy pulled up to a stop light and laughed. "I wasn't born yesterday, honey. Besides, that part's none of my business."

Gillian didn't say anything, but out of the corner of her eye she saw Dorothy turn and look at her.

"Oh," Dorothy said quietly. "You're serious."

Gillian smiled. "It's because of me," she said.

"Well I could've guessed that."

"I almost married a philanderer once." Gillian explained her misgivings about being used and discarded. She didn't know why she told Dorothy about any of it, except that Dorothy was easy to talk to. "I'm not rushing this time."

"Good for you. It's good to have standards in this business."

"Thanks," Gillian said, feeling for the first time like she wasn't completely crazy for not jumping into Will's bed, even if she wanted to.

‌‌‌‌‌‌‌‌‌‌‌‌‌‌‌‌‌‌‌‌‌‌‌‌‌‌‌‌‌‌‌‌‌‌‌‌‌‌‌‌‌‌‌‌‌‌‌‌‌‌‌‌‌‌‌‌‌‌‌‌‌‌‌‌‌‌‌‌‌‌‌‌‌‌‌‌‌‌‌‌‌‌‌‌‌‌‌‌‌‌‌‌‌‌‌‌‌‌‌‌‌‌‌‌‌‌‌‌‌‌‌‌‌‌‌‌‌‌‌‌‌‌‌‌‌‌‌‌‌‌‌‌‌‌‌‌‌‌‌‌‌‌‌‌‌‌‌‌‌‌‌‌‌‌‌‌‌‌‌‌‌‌‌‌‌‌‌‌‌‌‌ ‌‌‌‌‌‌‌‌‌‌‌‌‌‌‌‌‌‌‌‌‌‌‌‌‌‌‌ ﻬﻬ

They parked a good distance from the entrance. Gillian gave herself one more look in the visor's mirror and snapped it shut. She felt giddy, not sure she could walk all the way to the building. At least she wouldn't wobble like a marionette this time, she thought ruefully.

"Now don't you be nervous," Dorothy said. "Imagine you're back at The Blue Fiddle, singing around all your old friends."

Sadly, she'd had to quit both her waitressing jobs at The Blue Fiddle and The Sweetest Tea because she was too busy with everything else. The agency was generously funding a bunch of her needs that she would pay back when she started earning enough money from her music, even though she had a hunch a lot of it was coming out of Will's pocket. She'd even given in to Will and moved into another apartment with Tasha in a little bit better neighborhood, much to Tasha's delight.

Truth be told, Gillian felt horrible about all the extra things. So far, because of her expenses and not having a recording contract, she hadn't earned Adams Music enough to make a profit. She hoped this meeting today would turn out to be something.

Dorothy's advice was well-timed. This blossoming romance with Will had been distracting her up until now, but Gillian couldn't forget her rule of not letting love steal her focus from her goals. She'd already bent the rules enough, but only because she felt as if she'd ignite into flames every time she got near him.

And *that* was exactly the kind of thing she shouldn't be thinking about when she was about to step into a meeting with Will and a bunch of people who might give her a record deal.

"Will's just my agent today," she told Dorothy. "I promise."

"Good girl."

※

When Gillian walked in, composed and unruffled, at least on the outside, Will's eyes filled with what Gillian had come to think of as the he's-dying-to-kiss-me-right-now look, but he quickly recovered in order to introduce her to the panel of people sitting around the table. Dorothy and Gillian were the only women in the room, and she was suddenly happy to have Dorothy with her.

Will pulled a chair out for Gillian, and as she brushed past him to sit down, his hand briefly touched her hip. Little butterflies went wild in her chest, a combination of the thrill of meeting at a record label's office and the idea that Will would dare touch her in the presence of anyone else. Nobody would have noticed given the angle they were at, but it reminded her that Will was playing with fire too, and he seemed to like it.

Concentrate on the meeting, she told herself. He's not your boyfriend. He's your agent.

"Play something for us," one of the executives said. Dorothy smiled encouragement. She didn't look at Will.

They didn't waste any time getting to the point, she realized, so she didn't either. She pulled out her guitar and launched into something she'd played for Will in his office. Will had given her a list of songs to sing and the order to sing them in if she got a chance.

It felt good to be behind her guitar, no matter how important the people watching her were. The guitar was like a shield between her and the world, giving her a chance to be herself, to express her deepest feelings on her own terms. It usually didn't take her long to get lost in the songs, and as she played, the room was quiet. She even stopped thinking about Will. It was just her, the guitar, and the dream she and her momma had been sharing her whole life.

She was startled when she opened her eyes in the middle of a song to find everyone staring at her. The feeling was more intense than usual with no lights or space between herself and them. She flushed. It was like singing naked in front of strangers. If they knew anything about music, and they did, they'd see every one of her flaws, her hesitations, her mess-ups, but she didn't let herself think about that. Instead, she closed her eyes and went to a different place, and it wasn't The Ryman.

In her mind, she was home in Gold Creek Gap, sitting on her momma's front porch in the cool evening breeze, surrounded by an array of potted flowers and darting hummingbirds dipping in and out of the blossoms, as well as the colorful feeders hanging all around.

When she opened her eyes again, the music executives were looking at her like she was chocolate cake and they were dying to take a bite. She might have been shy when it came to her talent, but she had enough experience to see that they must have loved her songs.

Will took over. He was a master at selling his clients, and she liked watching him do it. Gillian had learned fast that his charisma and confidence weren't just a show he put on for women. It was real and incredibly sexy. The whole time he talked, Gillian distracted her nervous self by imagining him kissing her, which was ridiculous of course. She'd just walked through halls lined with more gold records on the walls than she could ever imagine and now sat in a fancy boardroom with a bunch of music industry execs—possibly about to sign her own record deal—and after promising Dorothy she'd keep her mind on the meeting, almost all she could think about were Will's lips on her mouth, on her neck, on—

"Gillian?" Dorothy was saying. "What do you think of that offer?"

Gillian glanced at Will, noting the slightest smile tugging at the corners of his lips. Thank heavens he was able to concentrate. This was his realm, not hers.

"It's a good offer," he said, looking at her. Even though he'd handed her off to Dorothy, she'd spent hours and hours of personal time with him since then, enough to read him pretty well. This was his trust-me-I've-got-this-covered look.

"OK," Gillian said. Will smiled broadly, and Dorothy patted her shoulder. She'd obviously said the right thing.

It wasn't until they pushed a contract and a pen across the table that Gillian flipped through and saw a few figures and several of her song titles within the pages that reality hit. She wasn't sure why, but she stood up, and the trembling started before she could stop it.

Will stood beside her. Between him and Dorothy, they got her to sit back down.

"What's wrong?"

Gillian knew she looked like an idiot, but she couldn't help it. She turned to him.

"I want my momma." She smiled apologetically.

Everyone else burst into laughter, but when they saw she was serious, it turned into the kind of chuckles erupting from a crowd when a child stands on the stage and collapses into tears when they can't see their mom in the crowd. And Gillian's momma wasn't in the crowd.

Will turned to the executives. He managed to make Gillian look like an adorable small town girl whose mother got her started and there was no way she would be signing that contract until they got her on the phone. He whispered something to someone at the end, and they all disappeared momentarily.

"They're calling her now." He sat down beside Gillian.

"You had them do that for me?"

"Of course. Why wouldn't I?"

She squeezed his hand underneath the table. "Thanks."

The executives popped back into the room.

"It turns out your momma has video calling on her phone," one of them said. "So we're going to stream it to this screen here."

And just like that, her mom's face appeared at the end of the room.

"Momma!" Gillian broke into smiles.

"Hi, Ms. Heart." Will waved.

"Will Adams?"

"Yes, ma'am."

"Young man, I hear you're takin' good care of my girl."

"I'm doing the best I can. She's a driven woman, and you know she has a mind of her own."

"Don't I know that?" Everyone chuckled. "I'm so glad she found someone like you, young man." A long beat of silence followed. Nobody was going to comment on what the real meaning of her mom's comment might be.

"And Dorothy too," her mom said. "Is Dorothy there?"

Dorothy saved them. "I bet you're wondering what this call is all about Ms. Heart?"

"I *was* wondering. And please, it's Louise."

"Louise," Will broke in. "Let us introduce you to some of Gillian's new friends." He introduced each music executive one by one. Gillian watched her momma's eyes grow wider with each introduction.

"Now," he said. "They've offered this record deal to Gillian, and she wanted to share the big moment with you."

On screen, Louise was holding her hands over her mouth to keep from crying. Will gave Gillian a meaningful look, and her heart brimmed with affection. If that man asked her to marry him right on the spot, she'd say yes just for doing something as nice as this for her momma. Maybe he would've made sure any client's momma was live-streamed in the middle of a deal if they wanted it, but something told her probably not. It took her a minute to shift from Will back to the deal. Somebody handed her a pen. She noticed it was black and shiny with the record company's logo on one side. She hoped they wouldn't care when she put that pen in her purse later.

Dorothy patted Gillian slightly on the arm. "Let's keep it together, girl. Sign it."

Gillian decided she owed Dorothy a nice lunch after this for keeping her together. She'd been practicing her signature, something she and Tasha had been doing for fun. And with a scratch-scratch up and down and a few twirly loops, Gillian signed the contract that would make her dream a reality.

One of the executives, the highest ranking, if one could tell by the quality of his suit, leaned forward to shake her hand warmly.

"We're so very happy to have you, Ms. Heart. I'm sure your father is going to be over the moon. Isn't he?"

There was an audible silence in the room except for the small gasp from Gillian's mouth. She looked at Will who ran one hand over his scruffy chin like he always did when he was thinking, but even under pressure, he still managed to look casual about everything. It was only the blue depths of his eyes that ever gave anything away to her. She noted the concern in them now.

The executive shaking Gillian's hand continued to smile, waiting for her answer. He obviously hadn't received the memo to keep quiet about Cooper Heart.

She smiled and nodded, understanding the importance of remaining professional, even though nothing had ever felt more personal. Her heart had burst open at the mention of her dad, reminding her that he wasn't there, he didn't know, and he probably didn't care. And all right in front of her momma.

"He is," she said, even though she had no idea.

"We look forward to working with you, Ms. Heart. Who knows? Maybe one day you and your father might collaborate on something for us." He looked at the others for approval. "Wouldn't that be fun?"

Everyone whole-heartedly agreed, except for her momma on the screen. To anyone else, her smile might have looked like she had the same opinion as the executive, but what Gillian saw in her eyes was a determined message that said the same thing Dorothy had whispered earlier.

*Keep it together, Gillian.* So she took a deep breath and nodded.

Will gave her a sympathetic look, but she couldn't meet his stare. She wanted to be angry that he'd obviously made her dad part of his negotiations on her behalf, even though she'd asked him not to. But a part of her was all too aware of the truth. Dorothy was wrong. It wasn't the relationship with Will that she should be worried about when it came to work. It was the one with her dad that had the power to drain her confidence and topple her career before it ever got started.

# Chapter Twelve

Gillian hadn't said anything since they got back to the office, which worried Will. She should've been dancing and singing in celebration. The glasses and bottle of champagne sat outside his office door on Josie's desk, untouched. He hated how the executives had mentioned her dad right in the middle of the deal, but he had tried to warn her. The truth was, he wouldn't have done his negotiations with the record company any differently.

He was a damn good agent, and he'd poured everything, and a lot extra, into getting her a deal. He would've used Cooper Heart's name all over again if he had to. The suggestion of Gillian and her dad collaborating had been a surprise to him too, but it'd made him want to stand up and whoop. It was more than he could've bargained for, and any other client would have been elated, but Gillian wasn't any client. He was in love with her, and he sure hated the way she sat in his office right now, looking like someone had just punched her.

"I'm so sorry, darlin'. But you have to understand. Sometimes a small thing like that can make the difference between a record company signing one client over another. For all we know, there might've been another person in the race, and your dad's connection was simply the tie-breaker."

She finally looked at him, her eyes filled with sadness. "He's my dad. Our relationship isn't a story for someone to use to get their way."

"Yes, it is." He was matter-of-fact, even though he wanted to sweep her up in an embrace to block her pain. "And I used the story to get *your* way. The record deal you've been dreaming of all your life just happened, and I worked my ass off back there to get it for you. The least you could do is say thanks."

Her head snapped up. "You should've warned me."

His face went hot with renewed frustration. "Gillian. They loved everything about you. Did you know that even though they asked you to sing for them, they've already been out watching you at different venues?"

She shook her head, her eyes filling with surprise.

"Every time we schedule a gig, Dorothy and I let everyone know. Sometimes they show, sometimes they don't. They showed more than once, and they were this close to signing." He held up his thumb and forefinger. "And all they needed was one little promise."

"And what promise was that?" she said, her eyes stormy and gorgeous, but never mind that.

"The promise that your talent is real and lasting, because it's in your blood. By telling them about your dad, I promised them it was a legacy for you. And it is."

"I get talent from my mom too, Will." She shook her head in frustration. "I'm not ready to deal with my dad."

The problem was, outside of work he could listen to her talk about what a jerk Cooper Heart was all day long, but as a manager, he didn't have time.

"Gillian Heart, you aren't working this right. Get some counseling, call your dad and tell him off, cry into your pillow at night, but by all means, darlin', grow up, and think about your career."

She flinched like he'd slapped her. He felt like a jerk, but he wasn't saying anything he wouldn't say to any of his other clients. The only reason it mattered was because he was in love with her. Damn it. He leaned back in his chair.

"I need to grow up?" she asked.

He nodded, hating himself. "This isn't Gold Creek Gap."

"So, you think I'm some young innocent girl from a small town who can't handle any of this?"

He didn't need to answer. That's exactly what he thought, except she was no girl. She was all woman, and she drove him crazy, and it was making his job very hard at the moment. Dorothy had been right when she offered to take Gillian on. She'd warned him, and he should've drawn stronger boundaries than he had, but it was too late now. He couldn't rein in his feelings any more than he could rein in a storm.

He took a deep breath, running his hand over his chin. The sight of Gillian glaring at him from her seat reminded him of his sisters and his mom. They were kind and sweet like Gillian, but they, too, had fire.

"I'm sorry I hurt your feelings."

She sniffed.

"Forgive me, please," he said.

She swiped at a loan tear.

"I do," she said, and he let out the breath he'd been holding. "I know you did your job. And I'm grateful."

His face flushed. As much as he hated to admit it to himself, he liked hearing her say so. How many times had he seen her on the verge of tears earlier that day? She'd visibly struggled to keep them in, and now, thanks to him, she was about to leak all over the place. He couldn't stand it any longer. He shoved back his chair.

He was by her side in a heartbeat, kneeling with his arm around her.

"I was hoping that once you had time to think about it," he murmured, "you'd understand."

She took a shaky breath and squeezed his hand, and he took that moment to offer her what he hoped was a comforting hug, although it felt awkward with her stiff posture.

"Maybe," she said, "if you'd explained beforehand, I could've had time to get used to it."

"Would you have listened?"

She shrugged. "I don't know, but I'm not an idiot, Will. You could've tried."

His breath left in a whoosh. "I did, darlin'. Every time I brought it up, you were clear about wanting nothing to do with your dad, even to get a deal. Then, when this opportunity came up, I couldn't risk losing it. Time was of the essence."

"I have a cell. I'm sure you could've made time to call about something that important. You certainly have time to answer every single time Audrey calls."

Will stood and ran his hands over his face. "No, I don't. Not when I'm in a meeting with record executives. And the difference between you and Audrey is, she trusts me to make decisions for her on the spur of the moment. Negotiating is not for the weak, Gillian. That's why the clients aren't involved. That's why you have me."

She closed her eyes, then stood.

"Now, darlin'. Can we move on? Let's have some champagne."

"I know you're right," she said, her shoulders drooping. "I'm being ridiculous. I probably do need to see a shrink."

"That's not what I meant, sweetheart." He regretted

saying that, even if it was probably a good idea. He remembered all the times he'd approached his preacher dad's office door, only to be turned away because someone just needed to talk about things.

She gave him a resigned look, and he was reminded that even though she'd been living in Nashville on her own for a while by the time they met, she was still very sheltered. While she'd struggled with abandonment and being on the verge of poverty in Gold Creek Gap, the way her mom had protected her had kept her from having to be tough on her own. Everything in the past few months had happened more quickly than she could've ever dreamed. Maybe it was wrong to expect her to be able to handle everything at once.

"Come on," he said. "Let's go have a toast."

"Can we do it later?" She gave him an apologetic look. "I don't feel so hot right now."

He would prefer they celebrate, but he'd noticed she did look a little green.

"Of course," he said. "You've had a long day. Go home and get some rest."

He morphed back into her boyfriend and stepped closer to her, gathering her into his arms. She came willingly, much to his relief, but he still sensed uneasiness. He tried to relax her by rubbing her back, kissing the top of her head, pulling her close.

She reached up and kissed him on the cheek, and he sighed with relief. Maybe she wouldn't hate him. Desire opened up, and he wanted to take her home and celebrate in a better way, smooth away all her worry and hurt, but he knew it would only be a temporary fix. She needed more, and he hated that the only way he could think to comfort her was to take her to his bed.

"I think I want to go home and call Momma. I need some time. I'll be fine tomorrow."

He sighed. Of course that's what she wanted and

needed. Who can replace a mom? Smiling, he stepped back, putting space between them.

"Are you angry with me?" He hated how it made him sound weak, but he wanted to know.

She shrugged. "Maybe a little, but not really. I'm just sad. I wish Cooper Heart wasn't my dad. If my life were normal, this wouldn't even be happening."

The door clicked softly shut as she left, but the sound of it reverberated around the room and through his hollow heart. If Cooper Heart wasn't her dad, she probably wouldn't be in Nashville, and she never would've bumped into him in his lobby. He didn't like the thought of not having met Gillian, but he hated not being able to fix her broken heart.

He buried his hands in his hair and paced. He hoped Cooper Heart did come back to town soon. As soon as he saw him, he wanted to punch his face. He wanted to throw him across the room and hurt him for hurting Gillian. After pacing for a minute or two, he stopped beside the trophy case, opened it and grabbed the Grammy. He didn't know if it was because he was angry at himself, or Cooper Heart, but without thinking he flung it across the room, shattering the glass of a gilded picture frame.

Josie suddenly appeared in the doorway. She saw the Grammy lying on the floor and knelt to rescue it, checking it over to see if it was OK. She looked at Will with a sadness in her eyes that made him feel bad for the second time that day.

He brushed past her to pick up the mess himself.

"Don't worry," he told Josie. "I'm sorry. I'll get this." She left quietly as Will placed shards of glass in the trash can. Afterward, he picked up the phone and dialed a number he knew by heart.

"Fresh Picked Flowers," sang the cheerful voice on the other end. "How may we help you?"

"It's Will Adams. I need to send flowers."

"To your secretary, Josie?" He ordered often enough that they already had his information.

"She's my assistant," he corrected. "But yes, please. And also to one of my clients. Gillian Heart."

"She's new?" the girl asked. He rattled off Gillian's address.

"And what are the occasions? Josie first."

"For me not appreciating how she puts up with my crap."

The lady on the other end snorted. "And the second?"

"Apology."

"So you want the doghouse package times two?"

He laughed in spite of his frustration. "Is that a thing?"

"It is, Mr. Adams."

"Then yes, because I think I'm in the doghouse with everyone today."

"The package comes with roses and chocolate. Is that OK?"

He thought for a minute. Every woman wants roses, right? But when he thought of flowers for Gillian, he thought of something light, colorful and breezy.

"Can you do something really nice with daisies for Gillian?"

"You betcha we can. Something summery and lush?"

"Sounds perfect." Just like her.

# Chapter Thirteen

Gillian had always imagined returning to Gold Creek Gap one day in a limousine, surprising everyone in town with her amazing career, but on this day she had the driver avoid Main Street and go straight to Momma's house.

"Thank you." She handed the driver a tip large enough his eyes bugged. When she'd called Will and told him she was going to visit her momma for a few days, he'd come by the apartment and tried to talk her out of it.

"I need a break," she said from the doorway. "Will they understand?"

He'd shrugged. "I guess I'll have to make them." Then, he'd handed her a large envelope of cash.

"What's this?"

"Vacation money. Call it an advance."

"You can't buy my love," she'd said, trying to joke, but when he looked embarrassed, she apologized.

"Sure you can," Tasha had said, reaching through the

door and grabbing the envelope. She leaned in and stage whispered to Will, "I'll make sure she gets it."

"Gillian," her mom called. She stepped out on the porch dressed in a pair of blue jeans, flip-flops and an Elvis T-shirt. Gillian could see the younger Louise somewhere inside of that retro outfit and wondered how in the world her dad could've ever left such a beautiful woman behind. And how in the world had she managed to stay single? Choice, she knew. Louise had poured all of her energy into raising Gillian, and deep down, she'd never gotten over Cooper Heart.

Gillian looked around, happy to be home, as humble as it was. It would always be home to her no matter what, and it wasn't that bad. Many people in Gold Creek Gap and all over the South lived in trailer homes with pretty little yards and a cozy life. Her momma's lawn was mowed and edged. Petunias spilled out of a half dozen pots sitting around the recently painted deck, and hummingbirds flitted around, leaving a trail of buzzing noises that made her feel giddy. She'd missed the hummingbirds. The house itself was a little run-down, but it had a freshly painted look, and behind it sat Momma's small bundle of acres overlooking the river. At least she owned it all, one of the only nice things her dad had done for them.

"Are you gonna come here and gimme a hug or not?" Louise bounced down the steps like she herself was twenty-five.

Louise embraced her tightly. It wouldn't be the first time she'd helped pick up Gillian's broken heart.

She glanced at the suitcases. "Where's your guitar?"

"I need a little break from all of it. Even the music." Louise cast her a dubious look.

"Don't start, Momma."

"OK. Whatever you need." She turned toward the house. "And by the way, I'll have you know Will has called here three times to see if you made it."

Gillian lugged her suitcases up the steps. He'd called her cell phone too.

"He didn't want me coming home right now, under the circumstances."

"You mean, like you should be in town meeting with your new record label and doing whatever a new star is supposed to do?"

Gillian laughed. "That, and we got in a tiff, sort of."

"What happened, sort of?"

The floor popped as Gillian followed her mom down the trailer hallway back to her old room. Seeing it, she couldn't fight back a smile. She'd never taken down the posters of her favorite country singers, and they smiled down at her as she walked in. Frowning again, she gently touched a photograph of herself and her dad in a heart-shaped frame on the dresser, before snapping it face down. Louise made no comment.

"Will is the one who told the record company about Dad, and that's why they wanted to sign me."

Louise didn't look at all surprised. "That's how business works, honey. I'm sure he didn't mean to hurt you. He's in love."

"I never told you that."

"It was obvious at your big meeting. Even on my little phone screen I could see that the two of you couldn't take your eyes off each other."

Gillian cracked open her suitcase. She wasn't really surprised it had been that apparent. Her phone buzzed suddenly. Will. She ignored it and continued rifling through her suitcase.

"I bet he had a good reason for it, and I doubt the only reason they wanted you was because of your dad, honey. You know you have talent."

"It doesn't matter now, Momma. I just need a break. I'm going back, I promise." She pulled out a string of colorful western beads and handed them to her mom.

"Thank you, baby. They're beautiful."

Gillian just smiled.

"Does Will know you're going back?"

"Of course." But even as she said it, she knew he was worried. It happened to some Nashville dream chasers who couldn't handle the pressure, and they never went back. She, on the other hand, had signed a contract. He shouldn't be so worried.

"You hungry? I was about to make dinner."

Gillian wasn't, but she wasn't about to rob her momma of the opportunity to comfort her by cooking.

"Can you make me some real macaroni and cheese? I am so sick of orange powder cheese and noodles that come in a box."

"You betcha I can, baby." She leaned over and kissed Gillian on the head. "I'm glad you're home, but don't stay too long. Nashville awaits, and I want to hear my daughter on the radio."

Gillian grinned in spite of herself. Her momma would urge her to go back to Nashville until she repacked her suitcase, but for now, she needed home. After all the time Gillian and Will had spent talking about their lives, even sharing some of their deepest thoughts, it had been a shock to her that Will would share something so personal with a record company, even to get her a deal. But Momma was right, it shouldn't have been.

Even Dorothy was on Will's side.

"I think you're overreacting to this," Dorothy had said on their drive back from the contract signing.

"How? I asked him specifically not to share that story. My dad is a jerk. I don't want to see my name next to his anywhere in public."

Dorothy had shrugged. "Good luck with that. It makes a good story, Gillian. And your dad has written a lot of amazing songs. The connection can only help. I can't say I wouldn't have done the same thing if I were Will."

"It's just a sad story, not that good." Gillian's heart had been heavy with disappointment, even as she was thrilled about her record deal. Why wasn't anything in her life ever simple?

"If you didn't want people to know you were his daughter," Dorothy had said, "then why use the last name Heart?"

Gillian hadn't been able to think of an answer. The truth was, she'd asked herself a dozen times if she should change her last name, but she didn't want to. It was the only thing she had left of her dad's, which absolutely conflicted with the very reason she was feeling so frustrated. Dorothy was right. Neither Will the agent nor Will the boyfriend had tried to hurt her. Still, her heart hurt anyway.

"Momma?" she called, coming up the hall. "Do you have any coffee?"

She stopped short to see a huge arrangement of cut flowers of several daisy varieties in white, yellow, and purple she hadn't noticed before.

"Wow, you have an admirer?"

Her momma smiled from the tiny kitchen. "No, silly. Daisies are your thing, not mine. Those are for you. I guess you know who from."

"But Tasha said he already sent flowers to the apartment."

"Well, you can't thwart love, honey. According to Tasha, when he found out you were already gone, he told her to keep them and sent more here."

She plucked the card and opened it. "You talked to Tasha?"

"Sure did. What's the card say?"

"Asks the mom who gives her daughter no privacy."

Louise laughed. "You know you want to tell me."

Gillian smiled. She did. "It says, 'Darlin', I'm sorry. Come back soon.'"

Her mom's mouth turned down in the same kind of shape as when she saw a hurt puppy, and so did Gillian's.

## Chapter Fourteen

Ten days later, Gillian's mom playfully spanked her rump. "Now those are what I call a pair of jeans, girl. I wish they'd had jeans like that when I was trying to make it in Nashville. Are they new?"

"Yes, even though I can't really afford them. Cute, right?"

"Very glitzy. Shopping's more fun in Nashville," Louise said. "I remember."

"More expensive too."

"Speaking of shopping, I know what we can do today. Let's go to Caroline's."

"I'm too tired to shop, Momma. I just want to hang out here." She guzzled a glass of sweet iced tea, its coolness making her wish she could dive into a whole pool of it.

"In this microwave oven? I don't think so." Louise was referring to the fact that the air conditioning unit wasn't working again. "Get in the car. Caroline's AC always works."

As they were leaving, they were met at the door by the flower delivery guy—again.

"Hi, Joe," Louise said. "Thank you." She handed him a few dollars.

"No, ma'am. The gentleman took care of the tip." Already accustomed to the routine, he held the flowers—more daisies—out to Gillian. Her mom looked at her. More puppy dog faces.

৵৵

Caroline's was one of the little boutique shops on Main Street in downtown Gold Creek Gap. Walking past the simple, but charming, strip of shops on Main Street was the exact opposite of anything in Nashville. The town was humble, maybe even a little run down in places, and there was no music pouring out of the business fronts as they walked past. But it was a cute little street with hanging baskets of flowers spilling over with blues and pinks, spectacular magnolia trees in bloom, and clean sidewalks.

"I do love this place," Gillian said. "I miss it."

"Well, you're here now, no matter how many times Will has called to get you to go back." Her mom looked at her with feeling. "He misses you."

"Yes, I know. He calls me a jillion times a day, and I get so many texts I barely have time to read them."

"But you do." Her eyes twinkled.

"I do," Gillian conceded. Most of the messages were filled with words like "I'm sorry," "Forgive me," and "Baby, come back." It was only a matter of time before he called to serenade her or something.

A bell tinkled, and they were met with a wave of cool air. Caroline herself, still working at eighty-five years old if she was a day, came out of the back room and gave Gillian a pat on the arm.

"Well, if it isn't Gillian Heart! And Louise."

"Caroline. It's so good to see you. You haven't changed a bit."

"Stop teasing me," Caroline said. "You have. You look beautiful. Let's see what we can find to complement those beautiful eyes of yours. Something to impress your boyfriend? Your fans?"

"My fans?"

"Well yes. Your momma told us about your record deal. Congratulations." She motioned toward a rack of clothes. "Now shop. Have fun." She disappeared again behind the counter.

Louise giggled as she held a beautiful butterfly print shirt up to her chin.

"Gorgeous, Momma. It's on sale." She glanced at the price tag. "Wow! I'm buying this for you."

"Absolutely not." Louise hung the flowy shirt back on the rack. "You told me you couldn't afford the jeans you're wearing."

Gillian snatched the shirt back off the rack. "Yes, but you're my momma. You deserve one nice thing."

Her mom touched her cheek. "Baby, I have one nice thing. It's you."

Gillian snorted. "I'm getting it for you. No ifs, ands or buts."

"The only problem is," Louise said, "I have no idea where to wear a snazzy shirt like this. It's even too shiny for church."

"You should definitely wear it to church."

Momma handed the shirt to Caroline at the counter. "This one's for me, and *I'm* buying it."

Gillian shook her head at Caroline, who winked back. She followed Louise over to a rack of dresses.

"So, when are you going back, honey?" her momma asked.

"This conversation is never going to end, is it?"

"No. So when are you?"

"I don't know," Gillian said. "I like hanging out with you."

"I love hanging out with you too, sugar, but don't wait too long. You and Will are hot together, and now you're like two ice cubes stuck in an ice tray—and in different towns to boot."

"Momma!" She wasn't comfortable with her mom using words like "hot" to describe anything except the temperature of food.

"Well, it's true. You two remind me of me and your dad."

"Momma, can we not talk about you-know-who? He treated you terribly. Why do you want to keep remembering?"

"Because, he was the love of my life, Gillian. He was a jerk, yes, and he did cheat, but for a time, we really loved each other."

Gillian could have reminded her mom that he obviously hadn't loved her as much as she loved him, or he wouldn't have behaved so badly. He certainly couldn't have loved Gillian.

"Don't you regret having him in your life, Momma? Because I do." She fought the pang of anger in her chest.

"No." She grabbed Gillian's hand and squeezed hard to get her attention. "That's what I want you to know. I'll never regret your dad, because that would mean I regret you. I'm glad we dove in like two crazy fools and that we had the best journey up until the part about his leaving. I'm sorry he hurt you, and me, but I don't regret him."

Gillian, rightfully stunned, hugged her mom.

"You're the best, Momma."

"Maybe not." Louise hung a dress back on the rack. "If I were a good mom, I would've gone with you to Nashville, and then you wouldn't be standing here right now. I would've made you stay right there in Nashville and not skip your meetings with your new record label."

"Don't worry. I'm going back, just like I said." She hoped her label would forgive her. The last several days, the gravity of her snap decision to skip town without any warning had her worried. "You know I can't stay away from music, Momma."

"Or from Will," Louise said. She squeezed Gillian's hand. "I don't want you to regret Will, OK? And I don't want you to regret your dad."

Gillian gave a sad smile. She wasn't sure the part about her dad was possible, but before she could answer, there was a jingle at the front of the store.

"Gillian, dear?" It was Caroline. "There seems to be someone here to see you."

For a ridiculous moment, Gillian looked up, hoping to see Will, but it was only the delivery man.

"I was delivering something to Caroline but have something for Gillian," he said. "I could give it to you right now. It's in the truck." He motioned toward the door with his clipboard.

Gillian handed her purchases and a wad of bills to Caroline. "That cash is for Momma's clothes too."

Louise tut-tutted, but Gillian brushed it off. Her momma deserved some nice things. Ignoring the protests at the counter, she hurried out after the delivery man.

As soon as he pulled the large rectangular package out of the truck, Gillian knew what it was. The guy gently sat it on the ground beside her and held out his clipboard to sign.

"Do you want me to carry it to your car?"

"Oh, no. I can get it. Thanks."

"I bet I know what that is," Louise said, walking up behind her.

"Do you think he's sending me a hint?" The more distance Gillian gained from Nashville, the more embarrassed she was for leaving exactly one day after signing the deal. And of course, there was the wasted champagne.

"Oh no," Gillian said.

"What is it, sugar?"

At the time, Gillian had been in too much pain to think about Josie. But now Gillian remembered the bottle glittering in the ice and the sparkling long-stemmed flutes on the desk where Josie had sat, smiling, as Gillian left.

"I was thinking of Josie, Will's assistant. She had champagne and cheese all ready to toast my deal. I didn't even give her a chance to pour it, or to thank her for all she's been doing. I just left." Gillian shook her head, disgusted at herself.

"Well, goodness," Louise said. "That's not like you."

"I know. I'm so embarrassed."

"I bet it was the good stuff too." Her mom gave her a playful squeeze of the shoulder.

"Thanks, Momma, for making me realize what a bad child I am."

Louise laughed. "Just doing my job."

"I love you, Momma."

"I love you too, sugar."

෯෯

In her tiny bedroom back at the house, surrounded by more teddy bears than one might imagine could fit into a small room, Gillian arranged a fan in the corner and stood in only her tank top and underwear with her arms out to the side, trying to cool off.

"Oh, my gosh," she moaned into the empty room. "It's hotter 'n hell's basement on the day of reckoning."

Giving up on cooling off, she opened the box from Will, pulled out all the packaging, and lifted out her guitar. There was a note.

*Dear Gillian,*

*Tasha said you left this behind, but since you're taking a creative vacation before you get started, which is what I told the record label when they were impatient to meet with you, I thought you might need this to write some new songs.*

Gillian swiped a stupid tear.

*I Love You, darlin'.*

*-Will*

Gillian picked up the guitar. She'd missed it more than she thought she would. Adjusting the strap, she placed it over her head, her hands along the strings. It needed a little bit of tuning, but that didn't take long.

How in the world had she thought she could take a break from music? Especially when she'd signed a contract? It had always been her dream to make it in Nashville, and she was on her way. She only hoped her overwhelming need to see her momma and Gold Creek Gap wouldn't jeopardize her career.

Gazing out the bedroom window at her momma's row of hollyhocks waving in the breeze, she picked out a few notes, letting them hum through her body. It wasn't long before, in her mind, she was back at The Steel Spur playing in front of a crowd on the cusp of something big. She could hear the crowd go crazy and then quiet again as the sound reverberated through the room. The tiny hairs on her forearms stood at attention. She wanted to write a new song.

She wanted to write a dozen new songs, and as she wrote, her heart opened up as sure as the blue morning glories winding up the front porch. Her dad might have abandoned her, but the truth was, he'd left her with the gift of music. She was OK, and she couldn't wait to tell Will.

◆◆◆

Hours later as she was still writing, her phone buzzed with a new text.

*"What do you think of my latest present, darlin'?"*

She dialed his number. She hadn't used video calling with anyone except Louise, but she wanted to see him. When his face popped up on the screen, her chest tightened a little.

He skipped right past hello. "Lord Almighty, you are so beautiful. I can't wait to get my hands on you."

She offered him a smile. "You've always had the worst come-on lines."

"Who, me?"

"Yes, you."

"What else do I need to say to get you to come back?"

She propped the phone on her dresser and picked up her guitar. Settling on her bed, she hit a chord.

"I don't belong in Nashville, Will. At least not all of me."

He frowned. "I was afraid you'd say that."

"A part of me has to be here," she said, rushing to explain.

"Listen, Gillian—"

"That's what I've realized," Gillian said. "Since I've been home. Anyway, listen to this."

It was a love song, but not like the ones she'd been singing for Will lately. This one was about a girl who left town for bigger dreams, only to find out that what she wanted couldn't be found in Gold Creek Gap or Nashville. Only in her heart and in the heart of the man she loved. When she hit the last chord, she waited for

Will to say something. He didn't.

She peered into the little phone screen. Will was seated, elbows on his desk, his hands stroking his stubble like he always did when he was thinking.

Gillian held the phone close. "Well?"

A slow smile spread across his face. He started to say something, but his voice broke a little.

"Will?"

He placed his hand on his heart, shaking his head back and forth.

"Ms. Gillian Heart, I'd like to sign you on the spot," he teased.

"So you liked the song?"

"Darlin', I loved it."

Her heart brimmed with a crushing desire to feel Will's arms around her. "Nothing like the blues to inspire a new song."

"It kills me to think I'm the reason you left Nashville. Tell me when you're coming back."

"You aren't the reason. And anyway, you miss me, don't you?"

"You don't know the half of it."

"I kind of miss you too."

"Then tell me when you're coming back to be my client."

"I'll be your client." She smiled at the phone screen. "I'll be more than that, if you're asking."

He grinned. "Hell yeah, I'm asking."

◈

Louise knocked on Gillian's bedroom door right before seven a.m. on Sunday morning. Gillian's eyes felt like they were glued shut after another late night of talking with Will on the phone. They hadn't worked out every little thing yet, and he was still not ready to give up the idea of her moving in with him, but they both agreed she had to get back to Nashville.

"I love you, darlin'," he'd said, and she was slush.

"Oh heavens, Momma. I can't go to church. I'm too tired."

"Well you're the one who said I should wear my new shirt to church, so you're going. Get up."

Getting up early on Sundays was one of the things she didn't miss about Gold Creek Gap, but when her mom said get up, she had no choice. Soon the house would be alive with the scent of a country breakfast of biscuits, gravy and sausage, and if she wanted to eat, church was always a part of the deal.

"Did I ever tell you Will was a preacher's kid, Momma?"

"You didn't." She dished Gillian's plate high with biscuits and gravy. "Did his parents have to force him to go to church on Sundays too?"

"Sounds like it. Sounds like he was quite the bad boy."

"He's changed?"

Gillian thought of how Will treated her, all he had done for her.

"Yes. He has."

"Changed by love," Louise said.

Gillian's phone buzzed. "Who could that be this early on a Sunday?"

"It's probably Will, honey, telling you to enjoy church."

Gillian read the text and smiled. As usual, her momma was right.

# Chapter Fifteen

After the sermon, cookies and punch were being served in the lobby. It was comforting how some things never changed, one of the things she could always depend on in Gold Creek Gap. She reached for a pink sugar cookie shaped like a flower.

"Gillian Heart." It was Mrs. Wooten, her fifth grade teacher. "I sure wish I could make it over to Nashville and hear you sing something."

Gillian smiled. "You'd love Nashville, but I've sure missed this town."

Several women, many she knew from school, crowded around her. One of them piped up. "Why don't you sing one of your songs for us right now?"

Gillian looked around the full church. Hardly anyone had gone home yet. She smiled, touched, but reticent to start singing like she owned the place.

"Go on," Louise said, but Gillian shook her head.

"I don't have my guitar. I left it out at Momma's."

Mrs. Wooten patted her arm. "Please sing a little

song for us. Everybody wants to hear."

Gillian looked around at the expectant faces. What a bunch of nice people. When one of them produced a guitar from the stage, she gave in. People were starting to gather around. What choice did she have?

She sat on a stool that somebody placed behind her and strummed the guitar once, noting it was already tuned. "It's just a silly love song."

"There's no such thing as a silly love song," said the preacher's wife as she moved to stand beside Momma.

Gillian began to play, the notes dancing around the room in a summery, breezy rhythm that had the crowd tapping their toes and nodding their heads to the beat. Her momma smiled approvingly, and Gillian grinned back. She was having fun. She didn't care about Cooper Heart right now. She knew she would always be a singer, no matter how long her dad stayed gone. She would sing even if he didn't come back.

Someone started to clap to the beat, and she thought the only thing missing was lyrics more fitting a church gathering, but it was a love song. Love is everything, and wasn't that what they'd all learned about during the sermon that morning? She didn't have to work hard to remember the words, even though it was new. The song flowed out even better than it had when she'd sung it for Will, and as she watched the admiring faces of her small town friends and the proud smile on Momma's face, a memory of singing for those same folks when she was a little girl sprang to mind. They'd been her first audience, and here they were, still cheering her on. She wanted to thank them, so after that song, she struck up another, one they'd know the words to, and then another after that.

When she plucked the last note, everyone applauded enthusiastically. She smiled and was purposeful about thanking them for their support, as well as praising them for their cookies. She couldn't remember the last time she'd had food so good, not even at The Sweetest Tea where she'd told them she used to be a waitress before her agent discovered her. They were interested in hearing about that too, so with a nod and a smile from the preacher, she ended up being the focus of a question and answer session.

The sweetest part was when a little girl asked her, "Can I have your autograph?"

"You betcha," she said. "You know, I was about your age when I started singing myself. Do you sing?"

The little girl nodded, and soon there were a handful of children plying her with questions, and even one lovely teenage girl hovering in the background. She made a mental note to ask her momma who the girl was. Maybe she could encourage her, and the idea of it made something stir inside Gillian. Maybe she could be the inspiration for other small town kids to follow their own dreams.

Eventually people went back to visiting, and the children went back to playing. When she finally broke away from old acquaintances whom she'd wanted to catch up with, she gave back the guitar and headed for more cookies. She'd been telling the truth about how good they were.

"Gillian, dear." She felt a hand on her arm. It was Aunt Cher, who'd always tried to help them out after her dad left. "You are so talented, honey. Just like your daddy."

"Thanks, Aunt Cher." What else could she say? Her father was Aunt Cher's brother. Cher had tried for years to get him to call Gillian, but he never had. Gillian knew her aunt meant well, but she wished she'd just give up.

"My brother is a stupid man, but I want you to know something. The last time I talked to him…"

"Oh no," Louise said, coming up to Gillian's side.

"You didn't call him, did you, Cher?" Cher and Cooper Heart were known for the huge sibling arguments they used to get into when her dad still lived in Gold Creek Gap.

She looked guilty. In spite of herself, Gillian's heart skipped a hopeful beat.

"I'm sorry. I had to. He needed to know what he was missing when it came to his girl." Aunt Cher would have had no way of knowing the fresh pain her dad's name had caused her, but her momma did.

Louise slipped an arm around her waist. "What did he say?"

"He didn't say nothing."

Gillian wasn't surprised, but the news still hit her in the chest. He didn't even care enough to ask. Why would Aunt Cher tell her this?

"Well that no good excuse for a..." Louise began, letting go of Gillian and planting her fists on her hips.

"Momma," Gillian whispered, "it's no big deal." But they both knew it was.

"He didn't say nothing," Aunt Cher said, "because he was shocked, and then he started crying. I hung up on him after that. I just wanted him to know what he was missing out on, sugar. But he cried like a blathering baby, so proud he was." Cher smiled, her mission accomplished.

Gillian saw the look on her momma's face and knew she was trying to discern how this news made her daughter feel. She'd spent the last decade trying to protect Gillian, and her aunt shouldn't have called him, even if she'd meant well. Cher's timing was terrible as usual, no matter how sincere.

"Thank you, Aunt Cher." She gave her a little hug, remembering they were in a church, and turned to her momma, who looked like she'd been hit by a truck. They were both ready to go home.

But home, Gillian now understood, was Nashville. With Will.

"I can't tell you how good it was to see you with that guitar in your arms again, darlin'." She spun, shocked to hear Will's voice.

He was standing in the church's open double doors holding his cowboy hat in his hands and wearing one of his best black western shirts with the pearl snaps.

"How long you been standing there?" Her heart hammered. Unlike Aunt Cher, his timing couldn't have been more perfect.

"Long enough to see you sing like the musician you were meant to be."

Gillian nodded, thinking that maybe when it came to music, Will was the only one who truly knew who she was now.

"You crazy thing, Will." She rushed toward him. "I missed you."

"I missed you too." After a long, tight hug, he let go of her just enough so he could have a look around.

"This church reminds me of the one I grew up in." He reached for a cup of punch.

"It's kind of small," Gillian said.

"I like the small churches best," he said. "But they sure are hard to find in Nashville."

"About Nashville," she said quietly.

"About Nashville," he said. "We need to talk later."

A wave of shame swept over her, and she couldn't wait until later. She whispered so that only he could hear. "Oh my gosh, Will. I'm so embarrassed how I ran off like a kid. I'm an idiot."

"Not an idiot," he said, his own voice low. "But the record executives have been waiting for two weeks to meet with you, darlin'. They've guessed that your creative vacation is a sham. They're worried you won't be able to handle the life of a recording artist."

Her heart sank, all of her dreams swirling around with it and threatening to go right down the drain. Her happiness from the previous moment threatened to seep out as a stream of tears. She wondered what she would tell her mom, what she'd tell all the people she'd just sung for.

"So, they probably want to cancel my contract," she said.

"Not yet," he said, patting her shoulder. "Maybe if you bring them back some good songs, they'll forgive you."

She'd give anything to go back and not be so reckless. Leaving town like that was the stupidest thing she'd ever done. And over her dad! She shouldn't have ever made him important enough to destroy her dream. She gazed at Will, trying to gauge how bad it was. She had a feeling Will hadn't told her everything yet.

"What about you?" she whispered. "Can you forgive me?"

"If you go back," he said, his face serious. "And if you'll sing that song for your record label, the one you wrote about me."

"Only if you stay here with me today. We'll go back tomorrow." She twisted her face in a comical expression, knowing it might not be an option.

"Just today," he said. "Besides, I can't think of anything I'd rather do than stay in this charming little town, but you need to be in a meeting tomorrow afternoon if you want to save this." She could see he was totally serious as he reached for a cup of punch. He held it up.

"To saving your record deal."

"I don't think you're supposed to toast in church," she said in a half-hearted effort to lighten the mood. He touched his paper cup to hers anyway, then set it down on the table beside them.

"What about kissing?" He placed a hand on his chin, considering. "Is that allowed?"

"Only at weddings," she said, and then reddened. Hopefully he didn't think she was suggesting he propose, although she wouldn't have minded that.

His eyes sparkled. "Let me try to remember. I think kissing in church is one of the reasons my dad kicked me out, but come here anyway."

"Really? You still want to kiss me after I've messed everything up?"

"Mmm hmm." He kissed her cheek.

"Are you trying to get kicked out of church again?"

He laughed, studying the slight form of the smiling preacher across the church hall.

"I'm a lot bigger than I was back then, and I think I could take *him* if he tried, but make no mistake, I know how to be a gentleman around a girl like you."

He pressed his lips to hers, lightly, so as, she presumed, not to scandalize the church ladies. He pulled away, making a good show of being an appropriate gentleman. This, to Gillian's surprise, brought a few disappointed boos and some good-humored shaking of heads from the ladies standing around, particularly Aunt Cher, Mrs. Wooten, and amusingly, the preacher's wife. She caught sight of her momma, smiling next to Aunt Cher.

Will smiled broadly and said in a low voice. "I wouldn't want to disappoint the ladies, now would I?" Then he winked at them, which nearly sent Gillian's momma into a fit of giggles.

Gillian's face flushed, but she let herself enjoy the show, especially when Will wound a hand around her waist and the other along the back of her neck, dipping her low, and kissing her in a way that was romantic enough to prompt oohs and ahhs, and a few gasps, from the ladies.

Gillian believed he left them just a little bit, delightfully, scandalized.

# Chapter Sixteen

Will had talked Gillian into leaving the next morning, but tonight he didn't want to think about work. It had been a discouraging week. To his dismay, the record executives had insisted several times to meet with Gillian, and each time, he'd had to tell them she was out of town. After several attempts to schedule a meeting, one of the executives had asked Will if she was fully committed to a career in music.

"We have a hundred girls like her lined up at the door," he'd said.

"No you don't," Will said. "You know Gillian Heart is one of a kind, and she's got it in her blood."

The man had been silent for a moment. "All right, I'll give you that, but it doesn't matter how talented she is if she disappears on us."

"She didn't disappear," he told them. "She's visiting her mom."

"She going to see her dad while she's taking this little break?" The executive sounded hopeful.

"Maybe," Will said, knowing it wasn't really the truth, but it could happen.

"Monday afternoon," the executive said. "If she's serious."

"She'll be there." And he knew she would, even if he had to get her himself. That was the real reason he was there, to keep her new record contract from being cancelled, but for tonight, he'd decided, he just wanted to enjoy being with his girlfriend.

༒

"Dang. I've missed you," he said.

They'd driven to the back of her momma's field next to the river and spread a blanket in the bed of his truck. He couldn't think of anywhere he'd rather be right then. Besides, they were in Gold Creek Gap. There was nothing else to do, except play Bingo, which is where Louise had gone off to.

Gillian, a younger, even more beautiful version of her mother, sat beside him on the tailgate, her legs bare in a pair of cut-off jeans and a loose, lightweight flannel shirt over a white tank top. She looked content in the light of the moon, her legs dangling over the edge, softly singing some tune her momma had taught her when she was a little girl. Seeing her like that made him feel young again. How many times had he and his friends driven to the back of some pasture like this one and partied the summer night away? Of course, all the fun he'd had back in those days was a little bit good clean fun and a whole lot of his being a bad boy and corrupting good girls.

"This where you hung out as a teenager?" He found his mind going to the same place it had back then, and he grinned in the moonlight.

"Yes," she said. "But it wasn't anything like what you're thinking about right now." She reached down and took off her flip-flops, tossing them back to the corner of the truck bed.

"How do you know what I'm thinking?"

"Because I remember what boys like you wanted back then."

"Back then?" he teased. "Boys don't change that much when they become men."

She playfully punched him.

"Ouch." He rubbed his shoulder. "I bet they didn't get far with your right hook, did they?"

She laughed, the sound carrying across the river and echoing back to them. "I used to come here a lot, to think and play my guitar. Wrote a few songs out here too."

He watched her readjust the barrette that held her hair back, and the way the moonlight cast a glow around her face made him catch his breath. Without asking, he reached over and tugged gently at the hair bauble. She grew still, letting her hair cascade around her like a halo. Leaning over, he framed her face in his hands, kissed her softly, and then hungrily, the way he'd wanted to kiss her since the chaste kiss that morning in the church.

Not that he'd minded spending the afternoon with her and Louise, but he'd been wanting to get Gillian alone all day long. Now that he had her out in the back of the field, and in the back of his truck, his mind was running rampant with all kinds of things that might've shocked her momma and made Gillian forget her worries about her record deal.

Gillian kissed him back, meeting his desire with equal intensity. Her hand against his chest folded into a fist, balling up his T-shirt, and yanked him closer. Desire shot through him. Pulling his mouth away from hers, he left her gasping, kissed her jaw, and trailed his lips down to taste the soft skin of her neck. She smelled like some kind of flower, and he delighted in how she arched her back with a shudder of desire.

Her response made him ache with wanting to be with her, but reining in his hunger, he took his time. This was the boldest she'd ever been with him, and he wanted to enjoy it. Sliding his hand to her shoulder, he pushed back her flannel shirt and kissed her bare shoulder. It was so soft against his lips. Sliding his hand around the back of her neck, he tentatively trailed a line of kisses along one collarbone, tasting, teasing to see if she was all right with what he was doing. In answer, she tried to scoot closer, but they were already pressed up against each other, so she climbed over and straddled him. His heart hammered in his chest, and he gasped, grabbing her hips and settling her close.

"You don't know what that does to a man, darlin'."

"I think I do." Her words were a whisper on the breeze. She might have said she was afraid to give herself to him before, afraid she might get hurt again, but her eyes glittered with passion for him tonight. His skin burned as her tender lips tasted his neck, sending his mind spinning out of control. She pulled back to gaze at him, her chest rising and falling to the beat of his own heart. He slid her flannel shirt down to her elbows and drank in the soft glow of her skin against the thankfully thin tank top. He lightly circled his hands around to her back, and sure enough, no clasp. Holy smokes.

"Too hot for that," she said.

"Too hot is right," he said, taking her in. She tilted her head back with a beguiling smile, causing his breath to catch in his throat from the sight of her. His heart stirred with a different kind of passion, and he knew she had no idea how beautiful she was to him. He wanted to tell her about the plans he had for her, and how they included more than tonight.

"I love you," he said, unable to hold the words back. He pulled her close, reveling in the feel of her body against his.

"I love you too," she said. Her words sent a thrill through him, and he kissed her, wanting to drink in this night before they had to go back to the lights of Nashville. He was aching to touch her bare skin—the tank top was definitely in the way—but before he could do anything about it, she'd unsnapped and removed his shirt. The soft breeze raised goosebumps across his skin, and he trembled as her delicate hands traveled over his chest.

He cupped her cheek with one hand and placed his forehead against hers. "Darlin', you have no idea how many times I've thought about this."

"Me too," she said.

"But remember what you told me?"

"About what," she said, planting tiny kisses along his jaw.

"About this," he said. "This isn't you."

"What's not me?"

"You know, in the back of a truck without a ring on your finger."

"I don't care about a ring any more," she said. "I only care about you."

He sure hoped she was lying about the ring.

"You sure you don't want a shiny rock on your finger?" He watched her face, noting the turmoil that passed over her features. Her smile faltered for a second, and he knew. She definitely still wanted a ring. The knowledge quickened his pulse.

"It doesn't matter," she said, but he heard the reticence creeping back into her voice. He knew it mattered.

"You want a ring, don't you?" He wanted her to say yes, to know she'd say yes if he were to throw caution to the wind and ask her tonight. She took a deep, shuddering breath as he slid his hands slowly from her waist up her sides. He knew his hands were distracting her from answering, but he couldn't stop himself from letting his thumbs graze her curves. She was silent, except for tiny bursts of breath coming from her lips.

"Holy smokes, woman. Your body is beautiful."

He groaned, pulled her close, and kissed her hard enough to leave her lips puffy and red, then he made himself pull away. He had plans she didn't know about yet, so as much as he wanted to strip her down right there under the stars, he pulled her flannel back up around her shoulders.

৩৵

Gillian, in the heat of the moment, vaguely remembered telling Will the promise she'd made about no longer giving herself to a man who didn't want to put a ring on her finger, but the sensations throbbing through her body made her want to forget about that. Why had she even told him about her plan? But she knew why. The last time she'd done something like this, she'd moved in with a man and promptly had her heart broken in two. The memory of that pain, that rejection, set her on edge. And everything had been going so well up until this moment.

"I love you, Will. And you love me. That's enough."

"You sure?" He breathed in her ear, his voice husky. "You don't need a ring, first?"

Her resolve floundered, her head getting in the way for more than a few beats. Did Will know he couldn't give her forever? Just because he said he loved her didn't mean he could give her what she really wanted. Hadn't Robert told her he loved her too?

"Darlin'?"

She looked at Will, saw the desire in his moonlit eyes, felt it in his touch. Narrowing her eyes, she smiled.

"I'm trying to get you to make love to me, Will. Why are you making it so complicated?"

❧

Her words nearly undid the already loose rein he had on his control, but her next time had to be forever for her. She'd said so herself.

"I don't want you to wake up and be mad at me in the morning."

She giggled. "I don't understand the gentlemanly act. It's not like you."

He laughed out loud. "You don't think I'm a gentleman?"

"Not exactly, in some areas."

"Darlin'," he said, a wicked smile on his face. "Trust me. I am the most gentlemanly man you've ever known."

"See?" She could barely speak without laughing. "You can't even say that without exuding sexual prowess."

Growling, he leaned her back on the blanket. He couldn't resist one more taste of her tonight. Leaning over her body, he whispered how beautiful she was, and her giggling ceased as his tongue skimmed along the lacy seam of her tank top.

"I love you forever, darlin'." He planted a kiss right below her belly button. "You'll see."

He'd felt the surety of his decision with a jolt in the church that morning. Blame it on a wave of old-fashioned resolve from his days growing up as a preacher's kid, but in the back of a truck bed wasn't how he wanted his first night with Gillian Heart to be, or at least it's not how he wanted it to be for her. Truth was, he'd have her anywhere, any time, but if there was one thing he remembered his dad telling him, it was that girls deserved forever and a bed of roses. She suddenly gasped, momentarily distracting him from his plan.

Damn, but she tasted good. Something he did with his tongue made her gasp again, and he pulled back enough to study the glow of her skin and the shape of her gorgeous body in the moonlight. She reached her graceful arms up to wrap around his neck, her eyes filled with longing.

"Will," she whispered, and his lips were feather kisses across her skin, loving her and tasting her at the same time. She shuddered with desire, and he kissed her with more intention. A few moments later, he groaned like a bear who had lost his pot of honey, and placed a chaste kiss on her cheek. The rush of the river, the brightness of the stars, and the sycamore trees on the opposite bank reaching their leafy branches out in the moonlight would have been a good setting for what else he'd like to do to her.

"So you really love me?" he asked, taking a light-hearted tone but feeling the weight of her answer deep in his chest.

"Of course," she said, tracing a finger along his jaw. "Is that so hard to believe?"

"Yes," he said. "I can think of lots of reasons you shouldn't love me. I've hurt other women, tons of other women, for starters. And my stupid decision to press the issue about your dad, after you asked me not to, might have wrecked your deal."

"If my deal is wrecked, it's my fault."

"I'm good at wrecking things," he said.

"So you've told me," she said.

"And you've waited a long time for a man who won't make you cry again. I'm not sure I'm that man, but I want to prove to you that I can be."

She seemed to let that hang and then went back to the business side.

"OK, I admit I was naïve to ever tell you not to

mention my dad in Nashville. I realize that now. Being back in Gold Creek Gap has given me a lot of time to think. Especially about what you said about my needing to grow up."

He felt punched. "I'm sorry about that, Gillian. I didn't mean it. I was frustrated that day."

He gazed at her profile. She was staring up at the sky now, stars glistening in her eyes. She was a beautiful woman, and she didn't need to grow up at all.

"No, I'm glad you said it," she said. "It made me realize I did need to grow up a little. I've always been so dependent on Momma, even though she tells me to do things for myself. I've just always needed her, you know? Since I didn't have my dad, she became my whole world, but I need to believe I can do some things myself too. I do need to grow up."

"There's nothing wrong with how close you are to Louise," he said. "Heck, seeing how you treat her makes me a better man. I've called my own mom more since I met you than I have in the last year, because you make me realize how important my own parents are."

"I do?" she asked.

"Of course you do. And as for growing up, you left Gold Creek Gap and went all the way to Nashville by yourself. That's a pretty grown up thing to do. It's what I did, you know. It's what grew me up, at least a little."

He felt her soft hand squeeze his. "That's one of the things I love about you, Will. You know about where I come from, because you know about small towns."

"I do know about them," he said. "But remember. I'm the black sheep in my home town."

"Still?"

He smiled up at the stars. He knew most people didn't carry any grudges against him, not even his parents, for things he'd done as a teenager. His father had told him as much, but it was hard to forgive himself for those things.

"No, I'm not the black sheep any longer. I was just a kid back then, but I've still not been a very upstanding man when it comes to women. I'm afraid I have a reputation in Nashville too, in case you haven't heard. I'm the one who's needed to grow up."

"I've heard," she said ruefully. "Even you keep reminding me of how many women you've been with, Will, and I get it. You're so experienced, and me, not so much. I know you like women, and I'm a flipping twenty-five-year-old chicken who stupidly decided not to have anything else to do with another man unless he puts a ring on my finger. Except tonight, I wanted to change that."

"It's not stupid. It's mature and responsible. Standards are a good thing. I don't know why I never thought about that before I met you."

"Yeah," she said. "But I made that decision before I met you. You make me want to let go and have a little fun."

"And you make me want to slow down and do it right."

She stared at him, the corners of her mouth slowly turning up into a smile. "That is so sweet." She touched his face, and he felt a wave of affection for her that made him want to take her back to that little church and marry her right then and there. He pulled her hand to his chest and pressed it to his heart.

"I've had a lot of fun in my life," he said. "I never regretted any of it, either, until I met you. Now, I'd give all that up just so you'd never feel insecure about anything."

She turned her face to him. "Really?" He detected a hint of doubt in her voice.

"Darlin', I want you to know I haven't been with any woman since the day I met you, but if you knew about my wily ways, you wouldn't like it, sweetheart. Hell, I have one sister who isn't married yet, and if she ever dates anyone like me, I'll kick his ass."

She smiled. "I don't care about your past."

"You say that now, but later it will bother you. Mark my words. I've seen it happen to others. Heck, it sounds like your own dad had a past, and look what it did to Louise."

"That's because my dad didn't give up his past. And you're not like him. You're good."

"God, I hope you're right."

"I am," she said. "I know it."

He'd never had a woman call him good before, and Gillian had more than once. He found himself wanting to be good to her forever. He kissed her fingertips and continued to hold her hand to his chest. They lay like that in the warm night under the stars, losing track of time, and he wished they never had to go back to the city.

"So, we're leaving in the morning, right?" he asked, his voice breaking softly into the quiet night.

She was silent for a minute before saying, "Yeah."

"You're sure?"

"I'm glad I came back," she said. "Even though I'm sorry about the fiasco it caused. I could have handled it much better, but since it happened, I have to admit that being back here has definitely reminded me of who I am."

"And who are you?" he asked, part agent and part boyfriend.

"I'm a small town girl, Will. I can't leave my roots behind."

"I don't want you to."

"And I'm Cooper Heart's daughter, whether I like it or not. He's part of my roots, and they do run deep. I've figured that much out."

He was quiet for a long time, his breath heavy. He

was thinking about what she'd said about not leaving her roots behind.

"I came here to take you home," he said. "But if this is where your roots are, then—" He chuckled, but the sound held no happiness. "You can stay in Gold Creek Gap, and I'd understand."

She turned on her side to face him, and he was struck by the milky white along the curve of her cheek in the moonlight.

"Where do you think I belong, Will?"

"In Nashville, with me." He propped himself on one elbow, meeting her gaze.

"Then that's where I'm going, not only because I have a record deal to save, but because that's where you're at."

Warmth filled his chest, and he couldn't stop the smile that spread across his face. He knew he was no good for her, but if she kept insisting he was, then maybe there was a chance.

"So isn't this the part where you kiss me, again?" she asked.

"This is the part." His lips met hers with renewed passion, and he rolled her over on her back, gently pinning her wrists above her head.

She gave him a beguiling grin. "I thought you said we had to wait."

"We do," he said, kissing her shoulder.

"Then what are you doing?"

"Torturing myself some more," he said, before gently sucking at her bottom lip. He moved slightly over her, enjoying the warmth of her against him, wishing it was skin on skin.

"You mean torturing me," she said, her breath raspy. "Since you've already said you won't make love to me tonight."

"Mmm," he said. "I did say that. And I meant it." His

mouth met hers in a deep, wet kiss that made her squirm. "So be perfectly still now, so that I don't lose control."

He set to kissing every exposed inch of her again, which was delightfully quite a lot in that sexy tank top and cut-off shorts. A low growl escaped his lips. He wanted to be able to do this to her every night. What he was going to do to get her to move in with him was going to make Dorothy and everyone he knew do a double take. He smiled to himself. His dad might end up being the most surprised of all, and that gave him a good feeling.

He was kissing her down one leg and nibbling at an ankle when he suddenly pulled back from her and smacked his lips. "The insect repellent is a nice touch."

She laughed, letting him smooth her hair back from her eyes. "The ankles are targets for chigger bites around here, but I bought the kind that smells good."

"It does," he admitted. "But it doesn't taste that good."

She giggled. He rolled back to look at the stars. "It's peaceful here. I think I could get used to this life, minus the chiggers."

"I'm planning to visit a lot more often," she said. "You could come here with me. It's a good place to think."

"Apparently it's a good place to write songs too."

"It is that. Hey, when are you going to write a new song yourself, cowboy?"

He pulled her over on top of him.

"How about right now?"

# Chapter Seventeen

"Gillian Heart!" June rushed up to Gillian and Will as they entered The Sweetest Tea Café. "Welcome back. Where have you been?"

Gillian hugged June. "Back home to see my momma."

"Now that's a good thing." June ushered them back to the VIP room. "Tasha will be by in a minute."

It always gave Gillian a bit of a rush to sit in the back room with Will and the other movers and shakers of Nashville. How strange that she used to be one of the waitresses.

"Honey, you can't run out on me like that." Tasha poured them each a cup of coffee. "I can't be expected to feed Loretta forever, you know."

"Oh, thank you." Gillian had missed her goldfish, even though she'd known Loretta was in good hands.

Will pointed to a black and white photo hanging next to their booth. "One of these days,

June is going to be putting a picture of you and me

on this wall."

"If I didn't mess anything up. And besides, you're already on this wall with Audrey."

"Yeah, but I'm just the guy in the background. I might as well be carrying her purse."

"Ha! Don't you ever dare do that."

"Well, if she keeps making me money, I'll carry her purse all she wants me to. I'll be carrying yours too, someday soon." He grinned.

"You're crazy," Gillian said. "But you're my kinda crazy."

"There she is," someone called. Gillian turned to see two of the record executives from when she'd signed her contract.

Scooting out of the booth, she smiled and stuck out her hand for both of them to shake.

Once they all were seated, she cleared her throat and waited for one of them to speak. They seemed to be mute.

Will broke the silence. "Let's start by expressing how much Gillian wants this deal."

One of the men held up a finger to stop Will, and Gillian's heart twisted. This was the moment, she just knew, when it would all be over. Next they'd be pulling out the contract and ripping it up—or whatever they did to cancel one.

"We appreciate where you're coming from, Will, but we'd like to hear from Ms. Heart."

Gillian's stomach clenched. Maybe she still had a chance. She took a breath, tried to think about what her momma would tell her to say, what Will had coached her to say. In the end though, all she could do was show them her heart.

"I am deeply sorry," she said. "And very embarrassed. I have childhood issues with my dad that I've never gotten over. Your mentioning a collaboration with him shocked me. And honestly, even though I knew it was coming, just the offer of a contract was a shock."

She gave them a questioning look, hoping one of them would give her some insight into what they were thinking, but they both sat quietly, their faces passive.

She cleared her throat. "You see, I learned while I was back in Gold Creek Gap, that's my hometown, that I belong in a small town. That's where I learned to sing, where I went to church, and while my house was tiny and my mom was almost poor, I was happy there. I may be back in Nashville, but a part of me has to stay there, always."

"Are you saying you want to live in Gold Creek Gap?" one of them asked.

"No," she said. "Well, maybe sometimes. But what I mean is it has to be a part of me, in my songs, in whatever you have planned for me. My dad, I realize, will somehow be part of that too, because he's had a big influence on me, but maybe not in the way you're hoping."

They were nodding, and she hoped it was a good sign. "What I'm saying is that you signed me to this deal, and if you're hoping my dad will magically appear and be part of that? Well, it's never going to happen, but you can keep hoping right along with me if you want. In the meantime, you've got me all by myself, if you still want me."

Will reached out and squeezed her hand, not bothering to hide it from the men sitting across from them.

"We'll be right back." They excused themselves and walked out through the curtain.

"I'm so proud of you," Will said. "I had no idea you were going to say that, about your dad."

"Me neither," she said. "But I realized it's true."

"Good for you."

"But what if they don't want me any more? What if I said the wrong thing?"

He smiled. "I'll be here for you, darlin', whether they cancel or not. Someone's going to want you. I just know it."

"But what if *they* don't?" The little bit of coffee she'd had threatened to find its way back out.

"Don't worry. I'll always want you." He squeezed her hand again, and she thought that maybe, just maybe, that would be enough.

"Oh," she said. "Here they come." She sat up a little straighter, and so did Will.

One of them smiled. "We're all good, Gillian. We are still looking forward to working with you."

She felt Will relax beside her, while her stomach did flip-flops.

"Oh, my gosh," she said. "Thank you. Thank you so much."

After they were gone, Tasha hurried over to the booth.

"All is well," Gillian said, a grin pasted on her face. Tasha squealed, and Gillian was reminded that besides her mom, and now Will, Tasha was her best friend. She hoped with all her heart that Tasha would get her own dream someday.

"We have to celebrate," she said.

"We will," Gillian promised.

# Chapter Eighteen

"Would you like to see my house in Brentwood?"

Her heart gave a little flutter. Last time he'd asked her to see his house, it was to move in, and she'd made it perfectly clear she didn't want to live casually with a man. Since then, she might not have changed her mind about the living together part, but she wouldn't turn down a visit.

"I want you to see it," he added.

"Today?"

"Right now." If Will was willing to skip out on work for the day, she knew he was serious. And truth be told, she was dying to see his house.

"Let's do it," Gillian said. "Besides, if we are all the way over in Brentwood, it's easier to ignore the world, right?"

"Right, because you're about to see my world, sweetheart."

"Do you realize how conceited that sounds?"

He shrugged. "You don't want to see my world?"

"I do," she said with a smile. "I really, really do."

She tried not to gasp as they drove up the long drive through a yard as big as her momma's back pasture. It rambled and wound all the way up to a beautiful antebellum-style home with majestic columns, a huge front porch, and more windows than she could count. Around the house stood the most magnificent magnolia trees she'd ever seen, with huge gorgeous blossoms. Her favorites.

"You live *here*?"

"When I'm not sleeping at my office, yes."

"You sleep at your office when you could be sleeping here?"

He laughed. "Not every night. It's beautiful here, but there's never anyone around. It's kind of lonely sometimes."

It made Gillian sad to think of Will living there all by himself.

"This is stunning." She was amazed he'd been so humble about his house. All this time she'd thought he was only joking when he said it was mansion-like. It actually was a mansion.

"Why would you buy a big house like this for one person?"

He led her up the front steps, across the painted white porch, and to the big yellow door. "I guess I always thought that by now I'd have a wife and kids to share it with."

She couldn't help the little flip-flop in her stomach. She'd never been a gold digger, but she couldn't help it if the man she was falling deeper in love with had a house like this. Was this why he was showing it to her? Was he trying to tell her something?

"You want kids?"

"I used to," he said. "That's what I thought a long time ago, but the right girl never came along." He turned away to unlock the door.

Her heart dropped a little. Of course. It was silly of her to think she was the right girl or that he was bringing her here to tell her something. Will wouldn't be thinking about marrying a little ol' small town girl like her. She would never fit in a big house like this anyway.

"Do you want to go inside?"

"Yes." Despite what he'd said about the right girl not coming along to share it, she felt giddy about seeing the inside. Was it silly of her to pretend? She supposed so, but she couldn't help it. She was only human, after all.

He swung the door open. She gingerly stepped over the threshold and into a wide space filled with plush sofas, crisp white curtains and heavy dark furniture. It was a nice home, dearly in need of some feminine attention. Sweeping her eyes over the stark furnishings, she imagined it being her feminine touch that could liven up the place. Floral curtains, colorful cushions and vases of fresh flowers would brighten it up, give it a homey feel.

Will caught her arm and whispered in her ear, as if the house was filled with people who might hear.

"So you like horses?"

"I love them. My dad and I used to ride before, well, you know."

"Then let me show you the barn."

He walked her through the house, past closed doors she wanted so badly to peek into, and through the kitchen that made her want to hang some lacy curtains and whip up a batch of her momma's macaroni and cheese.

They walked out a back door and across a perfectly manicured yard filled with gardenias, lilacs and, holy cow, wisteria climbing across trellises.

"How do you take care of this?" she asked, curious about who had the green thumb.

"My mom designed it, and she planted a lot of it herself, but I have a service take care of it for me."

What a waste, she thought. "If this were my yard, I'd want to be in it every day. I'd have coffee on the deck every single morning before going to work."

"Would you?" he asked, without looking back.

"I would."

The barn came into view, and her eyes widened. It was bright red and big enough to live in. The corrals were empty.

"I don't see any horses," she said, disappointed. "I thought you wanted to show me horses."

"I said the barn. There's nobody here to take care of horses," he said. "I could hire someone, but horses need love and attention, don't you think?"

She nodded. "Gotcha. I agree, they do." But it was still sad.

"Too bad, though," he said. "Big ol' barn and big ol' house going to waste. Big ol' bedroom too."

She punched him in the arm. "Men will do anything to get a woman to go to bed with them, won't they?"

"That depends on what anything is, darlin'. I already asked you to move in with me." He was leaning on the fence rail dressed casually in jeans, boots, an old T-shirt and baseball cap. She liked when he dressed like that. It was as if shedding his cowboy hat and western shirt somehow shed some of the clout that surrounded him as a music manager. This would be the Will Adams that a wife would see at home, out of the watchdog eyes of the industry.

Her voice rose over the breeze that swept through the corral and lifted her hair around her face. "I told you, living together isn't for me."

"Yes, you did," he said.

She stood there, staring at him, her heart confused, wishing he'd say something to put her mind at ease. Something that would explain why he wanted to bring her to this house, and then act all nonchalant like they weren't both burning to rip each other's clothes off right there in the barn. Was he that upset that she'd declined his offer to move in?

∽∾

Will stared at her, framed by the house in the background and the lush landscape of flowers and greenery. She looked perfect standing there, like she was already a part of it, and she would look perfect in his bed, although maybe not the bed he currently slept in. Maybe one of the beds down the hall in the rooms his mom had decorated. The ones nobody ever slept in unless his family came to visit, and even then, many of them had never been slept in at all.

"I can't believe you sleep in your office when you have this beautiful place," she said.

"It gets lonesome." He smiled, hoping she might take a hint that he was trying to introduce a bigger idea.

"Then bring someone with you."

"I am," he said. "I did."

She smiled softly, and he wondered if maybe she knew what he meant. It gave him hope, and he thought maybe he wouldn't wait to ask her what he wanted after all. Why not do it right now? He took off his cap and was trying to work up the courage to say it, his heart pounding like a steam engine, when she spun around and walked away. He stared after her with his mouth gaping.

She called back over her shoulder. "Anything to eat around here?"

He shook his head, placed his cap back on it, and

followed her, his eyes on that cute little rear all the way back to the house. He felt like an idiot as he hurried to catch up.

Back in the kitchen, she swung open the oversized stainless steel fridge door, and he wondered if she liked it. His mom had told him women like that sort of thing, but Gillian didn't comment on the fridge itself.

ॐ

"Oh, my gosh!" she exclaimed. The odor that assailed her nostrils was far worse than any of Tasha's forgotten concoctions in their apartment's refrigerator.

He reached over her, grabbed the offending container of unrecognizable food, and rushed outside. Through the window, she watched him jog over to a garbage can while holding his nose. She erupted into a giggling fit, which she was still doing when he came in. Watching her with narrowed eyes, he washed his hands and leaned back on the counter while she caught her breath.

"What's so funny?" The corners of his mouth twitched.

"Oh heavens. You just looked so silly. Who knew anything could ruffle your feathers like that?"

He shrugged. "You found my weakness. Bad smells."

"I'll remember that."

"So, the bad news is, no food. But believe it or not, they do deliver pizza out here. Asian, too. How about some sushi?" He picked up the phone, his face void of expression.

"Nice try," she said.

He grinned. "You should try it."

"I will try sushi someday, for you."

"You will?"

"Yes, but I'm craving pepperoni tonight."

"Your wish is my command."

While they waited for it to be delivered, he gave her a tour of the rest of the house. She was quick to notice that all the rooms downstairs were stark and undecorated, while the rooms upstairs were all gorgeously furnished and homey.

"Wow," she said. "These bedrooms are so pretty." To herself she said, they only need to be filled up with family.

"I don't spend any time in these rooms," he said. "But I let my mom go wild decorating them." He flipped on a light. "This one has its own bathroom, and it's the biggest bedroom in the house."

It was decorated in cool blues and greens with a plush king-sized bed, a mahogany Chippendale dresser, and sheer white curtains on a large bay window overlooking the barn and the corral.

"I think I like your mom already. We love the same colors."

"Good," he said. "Because I'd like for you to meet her."

She snapped her head up. Did he mean what she thought he meant? There was only one reason a man introduced a woman to his mother, and that was if he was planning to be with her for a long time.

Gillian grinned. "I would love to meet her. I take it she didn't decorate the downstairs."

"No," he said, guiding her down the hallway. "Not yet. Here's my room."

She peeked into a manly-looking but surprisingly clean room, everything in dark woods, black and very cowboy. The bathroom looked small, but she supposed a man wouldn't care about that. The window also overlooked the barn, and she could easily imagine Will falling asleep there after a long hard day. Sad he didn't have a woman to cuddle up to in that big ol' bed.

She'd like to be that woman, she thought, but not as a girlfriend. She wanted forever, and as much as he flirted, he was probably just teasing her. He wasn't a forever kind of guy—he'd made that clear in his dealings with women in the past, right? He said so himself.

"I see."

"But that's not what I want to show you," he said, grabbing her hand. She followed him back downstairs and to the back of the house. He flipped on the lights of a large open room, revealing a studio.

"Oh wow!" She could barely take it all in. It was a gleaming room, obviously built with musical acoustics in mind, and was furnished with a host of sound and recording equipment. She touched a shining fifties-style microphone with one finger as she passed.

"This is spectacular. Did you design it?"

He nodded, looking proud as a new daddy, but when she moved to study some pictures on the wall, he reached in front of her and snatched one off.

"That one's a terrible picture. I don't even know why it's there." He walked over to a slim desk near the door and put it in a drawer.

"Will Adams, what is that?"

She gently shoved him out of the way and grabbed the picture from the drawer. Holding it up, she wasn't surprised to see a picture of a young Will accepting a Grammy award for songwriting with her dad, Cooper Heart.

He rubbed the stubble on his cheek, his muscular arms working in agitation. "I forgot that was up there."

She put the picture back and adjusted it on its nail. Stepping back, she gazed at it, wondering for a moment about her dad. What would he think of her and Will? She wondered if she'd hear from him, now that Aunt Cher had called him.

She felt Will's hands on her shoulders. "He's an idiot,

Gillian."

"I wonder if I'll ever see him again."

"Do you want to?"

She shrugged. "If so, he'd better have a good excuse for what he did to me and my mom." She reached up and grasped his hands, pulled them down around her so that he was now hugging her from behind.

"But yeah," she said, after some thought. "I guess I might want to see him, someday." Admitting it out loud made her feel better than hiding it. She was mad at him, but after all that had happened, she'd been thinking about him more. In her heart of hearts, she guessed she'd always wanted a second chance.

"You don't have to hang that back up," Will told her.

"It's your Grammy. This picture should be on the wall. Besides, this picture has to be a sign. It's as if we've been connected for a long time. We just didn't know it."

He spun her around to face him. "Thank you for letting me into your life, Gillian."

Her breath caught. Was this going to be it?

"Of course," she said. "Thank you for going to Gold Creek Gap to get me. It meant a lot to me, and it meant a lot to Momma. She didn't want me to give up on my dream. It's her dream too, you know."

"I hope she knows I'll take good care of you."

"You are so sweet, Will Adams. How did I ever get lucky enough to find you?"

"It's not you who's lucky. It's me. Heck, I used to be like your dad, but you're changing me, woman." He planted a soft kiss behind her ear.

"Into what?"

"Into a man who loves a woman so much that he brought her out here."

Her heart somersaulted. "I have a hard time believing you wouldn't have ever brought a woman home, Will."

He laughed. "I'm not talking about that kind of

taking home, darlin'. I'm talking about bringing a woman here, to my home."

"What about Audrey?"

"I told you, she has someone, but I wouldn't have brought her here anyway."

"The woman you were practically engaged to?"

"I was never going to marry her, and I already told you we had an apartment in town."

"So nobody?" she asked.

"I promise you, I've never brought any woman here before except my mother, and of course Dorothy, who insists on bringing me her husband's leftover dinner in little containers. Sometimes I forget to eat."

"Hence the stinky fridge."

"Exactly."

She laid her cheek against his chest, wrapping her arms around his waist.

"I'd love nothing more than if you lived here with me," he said.

Even though his words should have made her happy, her heart fell. He only wanted her to be his girlfriend and live with him. He wasn't the marrying type.

"I'm not a gold digger, Will. I don't need to live here to date you."

"Well, that's good. Because I'm not offering you an allowance, darlin'. If anything, you're going to be giving me one if your career takes off like I think it will, Miss Record Deal."

"Stop tempting me to live with you!" She threw her arms out to her side, laughing to cover up her hurt. "It's all just so much. It's a fairytale, Will. It is so cliché! If I move in with you, my whole life has become a cliché."

*And all my dreams of having the fairytale husband, home and family will be over.*

"What's so bad about that? It can be your fairytale."

"I like fairytales," she said. "But I think our ideas of

fairytales are different."

"I dare you to find out," he said. "I want you here with me, every day."

She walked from the room, twirling back into the kitchen. "This is a castle compared to the house I grew up in. I don't even know what I'd do here."

*I would decorate it and make it homey is what I'd do.*

He waggled his eyebrows. "I can think of a few things *we* could do."

Most of her friends would think she was crazy not to move into a place like Will's. If she did, maybe it would turn into marriage, eventually. She'd heard of plenty of people who'd done it that way, and it worked for them.

"You know what, Will Adams? You're crazy."

"But you said I'm your kind of crazy." He smiled broadly, flashing those gleaming white teeth in that amazingly handsome face, and her heart fluttered in her chest. It almost felt like a fairytale.

Almost. At least she'd have Prince Charming.

"Has anyone ever told you how much you look like Keith Urban?"

"What? That scrub?"

"Well, you're better," she said. "But that's what all my girlfriends say about you."

"That's funny," he chuckled. "Come here."

She walked across the kitchen where he stood at the counter. He lifted her up on the surface until they were eye level.

"Listen, darlin'. I don't know what's wrong with me since we met, but I've been thinking crazy things."

"About what?"

"This house. My life. Even the stupid manly decorations in my room. It looks like a bull rider lives in there."

"It is pretty macho," she agreed, wondering what he was getting at. His mixed signals were driving her mad.

All the talk about her being there, but no proposal. No hint at a ring or anything.

"And I don't want to be out here by myself forever," he said. "I've been thinking—"

The doorbell reverberated throughout the house.

"Saved by the bell." She hopped down from the counter, grabbed her purse and jogged to the door. "Hold that thought. I'm starving."

She was digging in her purse for change to hand the pizza guy when Will reached over her with a couple of bills. The guy took them and left.

"I could've paid for it."

"I know, but you're my guest." He carried the pizza box over to the counter and flipped it open. He took out the biggest piece and took a huge bite, stringing cheese all over the place.

"Save some for me! It smells so good."

He handed her a slice, and they both sat on the counter top, the pizza between them, talking and eating until there were only two slices left. She teased him about putting it in the fridge. "Don't let that go bad."

"I can't promise that." He reached for a small rack on the counter. "You like merlot, right?"

"I'm really a chardonnay girl, but I'll drink whatever you have." She watched him pull a bottle from a small wine fridge, pop the cork, and pour two glasses a third of the way full. He handed her one.

"To finding somebody to love." He held up his glass.

"Isn't that a song?" She clinked her glass with his.

"Probably. Almost anything can be a song, right?"

"So, let's go write one."

"Right now?"

"Right now, in that big studio of yours."

"Talk about cliché."

# Chapter Nineteen

Will had started out as a songwriter. Later he'd become a manager because he was a good businessman, but his heart was always on the music side. He'd built the studio in hopes of going back to songwriting someday, and now he couldn't believe he was sitting in his own studio writing a song, let alone with the beautiful woman he was in love with.

How could life get any better?

Of course, he knew how it could, but he couldn't get Gillian to stay on topic long enough to tell her his plans, to see if she wanted to be part of them.

"Nope, nope," she said, interrupting his thoughts. "Wrong chord. It's like this, see?"

She strummed a chord and sang a few lines. It was pretty, like her, but something bugged him about it. He picked a few additional notes on his own guitar.

"What about that?"

"OK. Let's try it from the top."

They played in perfect tune with each other, Gillian

sounding and looking beautiful as she sang the lyrics of a song about a couple so crazy about each other they got married in a Las Vegas chapel.

"You know this song has been written before."

"Yeah, but not like this," he said, adding a new line that nearly made her laugh out of her chair.

She set her guitar on a nearby stand and picked up her mostly empty glass. "This is so fun, Will. This is the best date ever."

"Is this a date?" He sat his own guitar down and drained his glass. He wanted it to be a hell of a lot more than a date.

"What else would it be?" Her gorgeous smile made him want to kiss her, again. Thoughts of the night in the back of his truck, and how ready she'd been to give herself to him, made him restless. Not that making love to her was the main thing he wanted, though. He wanted it all.

He shrugged. "Seems familiar. Like we've been doing this forever, doesn't it?"

"Yeah. I guess it does. I like it."

He walked over to the sound system and flipped on a track. "But the only bad thing about it is, I can't dance with you when we're both holding guitars." He held his hand out, hoping to make her fairytale complete.

She stepped into his arms, and he realized he was turning into a total sap since he'd met Gillian. He wanted them to be like this forever. He wanted to give her the freedom to build her confidence as a singer, to be whoever she wanted to be, but he wanted to protect her heart too.

"I want to take care of you, Gillian." They were swaying to a slow song, wrapped in each other's arms. She didn't say anything at first, and he started to sweat.

Damn it, he thought. Why did he say that?

"I think I do a pretty good job taking care of myself."

"You do," he said. "But I want to care of you, and you to take care of me. Together."

"Now who's the old-fashioned one?" she asked.

And that was his cue. Throwing every ounce of pride he'd carried his whole life off to the side, he dropped to one knee.

༄༅

Gillian gasped. Was he doing what she thought? She nearly stuffed her fist in her mouth to keep from crying.

"This is crazy, Will. It's too soon." But a part of her didn't care how long they'd been together; the biggest part of her didn't care at all.

He pulled a ring, not a box, but a ring out of his pocket. It made her laugh to think he'd been carrying that around.

"This was my mom's," he explained. "My dad got her a new one, and so she gave this to me, hoping I might need it someday. I never believed I would."

"Oh, my gosh, Will." Tears gathered in her eyes.

"I know we only met a few months ago, and that I'm absolutely crazy to be asking you this, but I'm crazy in love with you. Marry me, Gillian Heart."

The trembling started, and he must have remembered it from the record deal contract, because he quickly shoved a stool underneath her. She couldn't help it though. Even if she'd been hoping for it all day, he'd caught her completely by surprise. She knew he wanted her to move in, and he'd teased about forever, but holy cow. Get married?

It was all she could do to keep from crying out, yes, a million times yes. She finally found her voice.

"My momma would kill me."

He shook his head. "I expected that would be your first response, but she pulled me aside and gave me a talk when I was at your house. I think it will be OK with her."

ॐ

He trembled slightly at the memory of the conversation in which Louise had told him he better not mess with her daughter's heart. She told him Gillian was a forever kind of girl who deserved to be treated like a lady, and if he hurt her in any way, he'd be sorry. Then she'd gone on to tell him how crazy her daughter was about him. It'd blown him away. He'd been sweating bullets too, since only a few hours earlier he'd been about to make love to her for the first time in the bed of his pickup truck. Not that it wouldn't be a sexy thing to do another time, he mused, but first, she deserved a little romance.

ॐ

Gillian couldn't imagine her momma saying such a thing. She was protective, and she had experience to back up why she was.

"Yep," Will said. "I promise you, she did."

"Momma knows?"

"Yes," he said. "She did tell me I'm too reckless. But she said you were a little bit wild too, even though you hide it behind your shyness, and that maybe the two of us together might be crazy enough to make it work."

She smiled, her heart about to explode with happiness.

"Oh. And she also said she'd kick my ass into next year if I ever hurt you."

"Momma doesn't even curse."

"I guess she does if she has a reason."

She laughed at that. "Oh my, oh, Will." She grasped

his shoulders. "Really?"

"You're killing me again. So what is it? Yes or no?"

"Yes!" she exclaimed. "Of course!" She held out her hand and almost fainted as he slipped on a diamond so shiny she needed sunglasses. She held her hand out to stare at it, gasping for breath.

"This was your mother's?"

He nodded. "Does that mean you like it?"

"It's gorgeous." And it was. It was the most beautiful thing she'd ever seen.

"Not as gorgeous as you." He pulled her close, kissing her long and passionately, lifting her off her feet and carrying her over to the swanky studio couch.

He smoothed her hair from her forehead. "Are you OK? You're a little pale."

She smiled, wanting him to know she was perfectly fine and the happiest she'd ever been in her life.

"Come here." She pulled him against her on the couch, sliding her fingers into his hair. She loved to do that. "Now kiss me like you did a minute ago."

The touch of his lips set her on fire, and she kissed him back with a desire that had been growing inside her all day long.

With some effort, she pulled away. "So you want to be with me forever?"

"I told you back in Gold Creek Gap I'd give you forever, and I meant it."

"That's good, because if I let you do what I want you to, it's going to have to be forever."

She saw the hunger in his eyes, and he eagerly bent to kiss her mouth, her neck, his hands caressing her until she was ready to give him anything. Finally, she knew he would never leave her. He was the one. Her forever.

She was tugging at his shirt, wanting to touch him too, when all of a sudden he sat up.

"What is it? Is something wrong?"

He sighed in exasperation.

"Yes. No. I don't know."

"What?"

He smiled. "It's a reckless idea, but it just might work."

"What might work?"

"What if I told you," Will said, "that we could take care of *this* tonight?" He indicated them and their rumpled clothes. "And you can have your fairytale too?"

"You just gave me my fairytale." She held out her ring for inspection. "What are you talking about?"

He strode across the room and grabbed his guitar.

"What are you doing?"

"Listen." He shook his head, smiling to himself, then started again. "This is going to sound corny."

"It already does," she teased.

"Bear with me."

"OK." She pulled her knees to her chest, wrapping her arms around them. She had no idea what he was trying to do, but it had better be good after interrupting her in her throes of abandoned passion with her someday husband. She hoped their engagement wouldn't be too long. Just enough to plan the wedding, but not years, like some of her friends.

He started playing again. It was the song they'd just written. She laughed, having no idea what he was doing.

"You're silly." But he ignored her and kept singing.

He had a nice country voice, and she wondered if he'd ever wanted to be a singer, and not just a songwriter or an agent. Their song was fun and romantic, a little on the silly side, and the second time through, he sang it with gusto, changing the words here and there, but when he reached the punch line where the boy and girl run off to a Vegas chapel, he put extra emphasis on "Little Nashville Chapel," and let the note resonate across the room.

She crunched her eyebrows. "What?"

"You know. Nashville has at least one of those all night wedding chapels, like in Vegas. Remember?" He winked.

"So you want to change the song to Nashville? Isn't that an Elvis-themed chapel you're talking about?"

Will turned red, and she wondered what was going on. Then it hit her.

"Oh," she said quietly, and then as his meaning grew clearer, she exclaimed, "OH!"

He nodded, sang the lick again. "What do you say? Wanna get hitched tonight?"

She laughed. "Are you kidding?"

He kept playing softly. "I'm serious."

"You're crazy."

"I already told you I'm crazy about you, darlin'." He waggled his eyebrows playfully, and his blue eyes twinkled.

She had to admit the idea charmed her. "But I want an old-fashioned wedding."

He kept playing the guitar, musical notes dancing between them like background music to their act.

"Let's skip the engagement. We can swing by The Sweetest Tea and pick up Tasha and June to be witnesses. I'll call Dorothy and her husband. She'll be fighting mad if we don't invite them. Come on, Gillian. Let's be crazy."

"Our friends will think we've lost our heads."

"Maybe, but I don't care. You're the only girl I want. Why wait?" He stopped playing, and she saw that his eyes were filled with warmth and meaning. "I want to spend my whole life with you. If that's crazy, then I am."

He reached for her hand and squeezed it tight. "Come on," he said. "Let's do it."

She couldn't believe this was moving so quickly, but she had to admit the recklessness of it was exciting. What if she threw caution to the wind? Would her momma be hurt if she didn't get to plan a great big wedding?

He tugged on her hands. "Let's go."

"But what about Momma? You didn't tell her about this part."

He paused, probably remembering how she'd wanted her momma so badly at the contract signing. And this was a ton more important.

"No, I didn't tell her about this part, but it's probably better to wait until afterward. Moms kind of put a damper on one-stop weddings." He pretended to wince. "Dampens the romance too."

She grinned, her eyes flirty. "If we do this, I'm definitely making you wait until our wedding night."

"Then we'd better hurry up, before I ruin your plan." He leaned forward and kissed her with renewed meaning.

She giggled, a surge of joy rippling through her. "We're doing this?"

He propped the guitar on its stand and pulled her close. "If you really want the big wedding, I'll take you back to your apartment right now, and we'll set a date. Or… we could get married tonight. However you want to do this, I'm OK. But why wait? We can do what we want. It's our life."

She laughed. "This is crazy stuff."

"And if it makes you feel better, we'll have a great big reception later in Gold Creek Gap. The fanciest thing you ever did see. Louise will love it."

"This is real." She felt the seriousness of it settle over her, not uncomfortable, but it definitely had weight. "This is forever, Will. Are we ready for that?"

What if he changed his mind a few months from now? What if *she* changed *her* mind?

"Gillian." His voice was raw with emotion. "If you don't mind having to live with a skinny, workaholic who has to go dragging his clients—and colleagues—out of the bar sometimes, but will take you to church on Sunday and love you to the moon and back, I'm that guy. What I'm saying is, I'd be the happiest man on Music Row if you'd marry me. Tonight."

She bit her lip. Was she about to do this?

"Marry me tonight," he whispered, his voice husky. Her heart pounded with an array of emotions.

Finally, she couldn't take those puppy dog eyes any more. "OK. Yes! You don't have to beg!"

He looked surprised, jumped up and lifted her into his arms. She wrapped her legs around him and whooped.

"Now we have to give our song a new ending."

He set her down. "Why's that?"

"Because they can't wake up in the morning and regret their vows."

"I already told you. You're getting your happily ever after all in one night. We can rewrite the song any time we want to, and we won't regret anything. I promise."

༄༅

"Does that mean I get Loretta?" Tasha was standing in her waitress dress beside June at The Sweetest Tea, one hand planted on her hip.

"OK. You get Loretta, as long as you'll be my maid of honor." They both exploded into giggles. "And I want visiting rights."

Tasha grabbed her hand. "You threw your rules out the window, and now you're getting married—to a hot cowboy!" She squealed, pulling Gillian into a hug. "I'm so proud of you, girl."

"Wait a minute!" June ran back into the kitchen and soon appeared with a pink box. She called out a few instructions to her staff and turned to Gillian. "You need some kind of cake, and I have cupcakes. And did you call ahead?"

"Um… no?" Gillian hadn't even thought about needing to prepare. The whole thing was spontaneous.

June set the cake box down. "Someone get me the number for The Rock-and-Roll Wedding Chapel." It turned out they needed a two-hour notice.

Gillian suddenly felt the seriousness of what she was about to do.

June grabbed her hands. "Are you ready?"

"Yes."

In the truck, June reached from the backseat and lightly punched Will in the arm. "Where's your Elvis costume? I've heard stories about this chapel. I've been dying to see it."

They were off to Dorothy's house next. She and her husband were enjoying a night of reality television while the kids were off at their grandparents' house. They seemed thrilled to jump in their own car and follow the rowdy group to the chapel, but only after Dorothy thoroughly cross-examined Gillian to see if this was what she really wanted to do. When Gillian said yes, Dorothy smiled.

"I didn't think anyone could have a shorter engagement than Roy and me," Dorothy said. "And you have to let us bring you some food. I know you'll be too busy to cook."

"And that's why you won't be delivering any food," Will quipped. Everyone laughed, including Gillian who blushed like a hot summer day.

❧

The chapel was all white except for the flashing red and gold lights trimming the eaves. Inside was a large entrance with crimson carpet and indigo drapes. They were met by a middle-aged woman with a vintage hairdo like Priscilla Presley's, even though her nametag just said Martha.

"Do you want an officiant or an Elvis impersonator to perform your ceremony?"

Will's mouth dropped open. He quickly deferred to Gillian.

"They are both licensed," she assured them.

"Then definitely Elvis."

June, Tasha and Dorothy cheered while the men shrugged. Gillian grasped Will's hand as Priscilla/Martha showed them to a waiting room plastered with leopard-print wall paper. It was, conveniently, a gift shop too. June and Tasha pulled Gillian over to a rack of veils. Giggling the whole time, they tried various ones on her until Dorothy finally walked over and drew the line.

"This night might be a spectacle," Dorothy said, "but it's not a parade." She selected a white traditional-looking shoulder length veil and settled it on top of Gillian's head. When she pulled it over her face, they all gasped.

Gillian glanced in the mirror. She loved it, but would Will?

She turned to see his reaction.

He looked dumbstruck.

৩৵৶

Will swallowed, trying to clear the catch in his throat. He let his eyes travel over the silky white shirt she wore with a pair of jeans that fit her just right and those same boots she always had on. She looked gorgeous as always, but the veil transformed her. It struck him with a jolt that she was going to be his wife. What was it about a woman in a wedding veil that could make a man turn all mushy? He couldn't speak. He crossed the room and took her hand, staring at her through the gauzy fabric.

"Beautiful," he finally managed to say.

He wished they could be alone, so he could tell her what he was thinking without the prying eyes of their friends, but as he was about to pull her into a corner, Elvis showed up. He introduced himself as Elvis. Will shook his hand. He'd seen plenty of Elvis impersonators in Nashville, so he wasn't at all surprised by the dyed-black hair and long sideburns, but the sight of him made the women twitter. They made an unnecessarily big deal about his snow white jumpsuit that was splattered with more rhinestones than Will had seen at The Grand Ole Opry.

"Thank you. Thank you very much. Now follow me." They filled out some paperwork, and Elvis reminded them they'd need to make a trip to the courthouse later.

Gillian grabbed his arm. "I'm going to be your wife!" She grinned. "Your *wife!*"

For a terrifying moment he thought his eyes were getting all wet, but with a sniff he pulled her close. He couldn't begin to describe the emotion that coursed through him, despite the light-heartedness of the Elvis chapel.

He was getting married, and he couldn't wait to get his bride back home again.

"Let's get on with the show. We're in a bit of a hurry."

৵৽৵

The actual chapel was surprisingly tasteful with traditional pews covered with red cushions, a brocade carpet running up the aisle, and a heavy oak pulpit in front. Gillian stood right outside the entrance door, peeking in as Will swaggered up the aisle, followed by Roy and Dorothy. Gillian giggled nervously at June and Tasha's antics as they danced down the aisle in their waitress dresses dropping silk rose petals. Elvis stood behind the podium, microphone in hand, crooning *Love Me Tender* in a soulful voice.

Before Gillian was ready, Priscilla/Martha gave her a gentle shove. She stumbled into the aisle, clutching her bouquet of roses with shaking hands. Will stood about twenty feet away with a broad grin on his face. He was awfully attractive in his jeans, boots and a white shirt. He'd combed that scruffy hair, but it showed signs of his running his hands through it, the way he always did when he was impatient or nervous. Right now, he looked both.

Behind the wedding party, Elvis, in a pair of gold-rimmed, dark sunglasses finished his song and guided Gillian to the correct spot.

"Dearly beloved," Elvis said in a pitch perfect voice that made Gillian want to giggle. He gestured toward the witnesses. "If anyone has reservations about these two getting hitched, speak now or never—their love won't wait."

Everyone laughed, but nobody spoke.

The vows were Elvis-themed: Gillian promised not to step on Will's blue suede shoes, and Will told Gillian she was his little darlin'—which she already knew.

"Then do you, Will Adams, take this little darlin' to be your wife?"

He grasped her hands, and the Elvis wedding trappings, the performance of it, fell away.

"I do."

"And do you, little darlin', take Will Adams to be your husband?"

She opened her mouth to answer, but before she could say the words she wanted to say, she felt the waterworks coming. Will's eyes grew wide. June and Tasha moved to comfort her, but Will beat them to it. Reaching under her veil, he took her face in his hands.

༅❧

Will couldn't bear to see her cry. He smoothed away her tears with his thumbs, remembering the day she'd cried in his office. That wasn't all that long ago either.

Had he been wrong to think she was ready?

"What's the matter? I thought you wanted to get married."

She smiled a little, but a small sob escaped her throat. She closed her eyes.

"Look at me, Gillian." She blinked, her eyes wide and glistening. Will's heart twisted with apprehension. If she didn't say yes, it would crush him.

Elvis handed Gillian a tissue. She turned away from Will, and let Tasha and June clean up her makeup the best they could under the circumstances. Dorothy also appeared by her side and placed a firm hand on Gillian's arm, seeming ready to spirit her away. Will's shoulders sagged.

It looked like all the women were in agreement. Gillian turned back to him, her eyes still shining, but the mascara that'd started streaming down her cheeks was gone. He had no idea what'd just happened, but her smile grounded him to the spot.

She took a deep breath. "I do… I do want to marry you." She turned to Elvis. "I do."

"You'd better kiss her now," Elvis instructed. "Before you run out of time."

Will flipped her veil back, wrapped one hand around her waist and the other gently at the nape of her neck. He kissed her with a barely restrained passion that left her gasping for breath. Cheers went up, and amidst all the celebrating, he leaned to whisper in her ear.

༅❧

Will's breath was warm on her cheek, sending little shivers along her neck.

"Let's get out of here," he said. "I'm ready for our wedding night."

"Me too." And she was, but they still had to suffer through cupcakes and a champagne toast, which wasn't too bad since eating a cupcake had never been a form of suffering in Gillian's opinion. And once they toasted their undying love, they rushed joyfully through a paltry shower of bird seed and out to Will's truck. Will and Roy shook hands, while Dorothy, June and Tasha hugged Gillian and pushed her into the truck. Will honked as they drove away, and when Gillian turned to wave, they were all climbing into Roy's car.

Will patted the seat beside him. "Git over here, little darlin'."

Gillian scooted across the seat, straddling the gear shift. She adjusted the cheap veil, smiling to herself.

"Was it a good enough wedding?" Will asked. "You weren't sad it wasn't some big affair, were you?"

She laughed. "It was a huge affair. Didn't you see Elvis?" She tipped her face to kiss his cheek before settling back into her seat beside him. "And it was perfect."

And it *was* perfect. She didn't want to forget a minute of it, so on her way home she replayed the whole thing in her mind, memorizing every detail. When they rambled up the driveway of Will's—no, *their*—home, the stars beyond the magnolia trees looked a little bit brighter.

Will put the truck in park and turned off the ignition. He smiled, and not for the last time, she was struck by what an attractive man he was, and a good one too. She knew she'd married a man who would never, ever leave her.

"Welcome home, Mrs. Gillian Adams." She loved the sound of her new name on his lips. "Stay right here."

He got out of the truck and met her on the passenger side.

"What are you doing?"

He lifted her out of the truck and cradled her in his arms. "Carrying my bride over the threshold."

"Wait." She reached for her purse and a small red Elvis bag.

"What's that?"

"A wedding present from the girls."

He kicked the truck door closed and easily carried her up the long flight of steps all the way to the door. She giggled as he fumbled with the key while balancing her at the same time.

"You know you can put me down for a second."

"No, I can't." Finally, he got the door open, and before he carried her through it, he paused. "You ready for this?"

"I've never been more ready for anything in my life."

He carried her over the threshold, kicked the door shut behind them, and headed up the stairs.

"Which room?"

She laughed, seriously afraid he might drop her if she didn't make a decision fast. She thought of the one he'd shown her with the big bay window and pointed toward it.

He nodded and shortly deposited her on the bed. Propping herself up on a pillow, she watched him, amused and suitably amazed, at how fast he took off his clothes. He stood like a Greek god, she mused, staring down at her. Her heart skipped a beat.

He smiled that sexy half-smile. "Get naked, darlin', or I'm going to undress you myself."

"Is that another come-on line?"

He headed toward the bed. "No, it's a promise."

She hopped out of the bed before he could reach her and grabbed the little red bag.

"Be right back."

⋙⋘

In the bathroom, she slipped the white silky nightgown over her head, letting it settle over her hips. The girls had bought it for her from the chapel gift shop, and it was surprisingly pretty with a lacy bodice cut low in front and not a trace of the Elvis chapel theme. She sprayed on a scent that she kept in her purse and stared at herself in the mirror. Adjusting one of the gown's thin straps, she checked her reflection one more time, her skin flushing pink with the thought of his touch.

Already short of breath, she opened the door. Will had lit candles around the room, and they cast a soft glow across the bed. He rose from the mattress completely comfortable in nothing but his own skin as her gaze swept over his body. Desire coursed through her. He was more than she could have imagined. When she gave him a shy, but inviting smile, he moved toward her.

⋙⋘

A flood of heat surged through Will. He wanted to pull her down on the bed and devour her, but he was transfixed by the soft glow of her skin in the candlelight. He crossed the room, his eyes wandering over the curves of her body, covered by the flimsy silk of her gown.

"Have mercy," he breathed. "You are so beautiful."

Pressing his mouth to hers, he drank her in, his head dizzy with the sweetness of her lips. The only thing that could compel him to stop kissing her was the promise of her bare skin beneath that thin slip of silk. He pulled his lips from hers, leaving her panting as he trailed feather kisses along the neckline, struggling not to pull her down on the bed on top of him before she was ready.

"I love you, Gillian." He spoke to her in between kisses, his voice husky with desire, his body aching to be much closer. He loved how she trembled against him, and he wanted to give her the world. Pulling her closer, he let his hands slowly roam her curves, finding the hem of the gown and slowly inching it up.

"Oh God," he whispered. "I can't believe I finally get to make love to you."

He was so turned on, he had to take a few deep breaths. He wanted her to remember this night for a long time.

"You're mine forever," he said. "Only you."

"And you're mine," she said.

Her words went straight to his heart, and he smiled to think of how she'd changed him so much in such a short time. He never wanted to be anyone else's. With more feeling he went back to working her gown off her, but inched the fabric slowly, enjoying the anticipation on her face.

She gasped softly as he peeled the gown up over her head. He tossed it to the side, so that it lay forgotten somewhere across the room. His mouth fell open. She was so beautiful, so perfect… so much that he wanted to touch and to taste. He told her so, over and over.

"This has to be a dream," he whispered.

He reached for her, slowly sliding his hands around her waist, restraining himself so as to savor the silk of her skin, the curve of her hip, and letting the full lushness of her drive him wild. When she wrapped her arms around his neck, melding her body to his, he pulled her tight, their lips never parting as he guided her to their wedding bed, trying not to hurry, but eager to show her all the pleasures he'd been dying to give her for far too long.

Her lips still tingled from his kisses as he settled himself beside her on the bed. She traced his cheek with her fingertips, letting his eyes search her from head to toe. She loved the way he looked at her, the way it made her feel open and unashamed to be stripped bare in front of him, body and soul.

She gasped as he cupped her breasts in his palms, running his thumbs lightly across her soft skin. How had they waited so long for this? But Will had been right. A ring on her finger proved it was forever this time, and it made all her inhibitions fall away. She boldly returned the touch, exploring the muscular planes and angles, all of him, in a way she'd never done before. She wanted to give him a wedding night to remember too, because this was their first time together. His lips moved lower, setting her skin ablaze.

Her words were a whisper. "Make love to me."

His only answer was his mouth pressing against hers, and with a low groan, his hands traveled the length of her, his lips trailing along the surface of her skin, her curves responding in a way that made her burn, and moving together they unbridled a passion they'd both been battling since they first met.

∽◅

Gillian woke late the next morning to find she was still in the fairytale world. Her eyes sleepily traveled around the room, the blues and greens reminding her she was in Will's house.

Wait. No. Her house. Their house.

She smiled to herself. This was crazy but real.

Her skin was bare underneath the sheets, so no way last night was a dream. She'd fantasized about what their first time together would be like, but her imaginings in no way lived up to the real thing.

"I'm married," she whispered into the room.

"Yes, you are, Mrs. Adams." Will walked in with a cup of coffee. He cast her a wicked grin.

"Gillian Adams," she said, cradling the cup in her hands.

"Turns out Dorothy stopped by anyway," Will said. "I got a text to look on the front porch and found all this."

She plucked one of the oversized blueberry muffins from the basket. "I love Dorothy, and I'm starving."

They moved to the bay window where Gillian sat wrapped in a sheet gazing out at the barn. "We're getting horses, right?"

"Anything you want. This big ol' house isn't going to be quiet and boring any more." He reached a hand out, squeezing her knee.

"Maybe some people will think we rushed things," she said. "But I'm so happy."

"You still think I'm crazy?" He winked at her.

"Definitely." She leaned over for a kiss. "And I love it."

"So, I was thinking about that song we wrote last night, before we got married."

She smiled. "I love that song."

"Just look how it ended," he said. "No Las Vegas-style regrets."

She thought about the studio downstairs and how songwriting had brought them together, how it had brought about their wedding, and how it would always be a part of their story.

She sipped her coffee, imagining the rest of their life together. She leaned against his chest.

"Let's always write love songs together, Will."

He planted a kiss on her shoulder. "I have a better idea."

She raised her chin, shivering when he planted a kiss

on her neck.

"What could be better than writing love songs?" she asked, but she had a feeling she knew the answer.

He trailed a line of kisses up to her cheek. "How about we live them?"

She relaxed as he wrapped his arms around her. She liked that idea better.

No, she loved it.

# Epilogue

One more missing piece in Gillian's life found its place, albeit after a bit of a struggle. Upon hearing about her marriage to Will, no doubt from Aunt Cher, Cooper Heart showed up at one of her performances. She refused to see him, so Will had to send him away. Only after two more tries did she finally give him a chance to explain, but through the crack of the dressing room door, her on one side and him on the other.

He told her he'd been wrong to abandon her, that he'd been a downright idiot by letting fame and money consume him. He'd thought he would experience a bit of the Nashville life, hobnobbing with all the famous people, and then come back home, but her momma hadn't let him. "I don't blame her," he'd said. "She only wanted to protect you. And I used my money as a bargaining tool, refusing to support you unless your mom let me back into your lives. I regret that. I was wrong, Gillian." Tears gathered in Gillian's eyes, but she wouldn't let them fall, wouldn't fall into his arms so quickly. She told him she needed more time.

Gillian didn't blame Louise. Her momma had done the right thing by not letting Cooper come in and out of their lives at his own whim. He would have been a bad influence on her, even if her little girl heart would've taken him however she could get him. She was no longer a little girl, though, and after a lot of soul-searching, and making her dad beg, she decided it was time to move forward. But only because it seemed her mother already had.

Louise had decided to forgive Cooper after he'd been one of the subjects of a big Nashville magazine article about the price of fame. Allowing himself to be interviewed, he was quoted as saying that the biggest mistake of his life was leaving his family, and the most despicable thing he'd ever done was to smother the light of his talented wife, Louise Heart, who'd never been given a chance to shine.

"Since my daughter came on the Nashville scene, people have said she's as talented as me, but it's not true. Gillian gets every bit of her talent from her momma," he told the reporter. "Louise raised our daughter right. She's the reason Gillian turned out to be so beautiful, talented and a good person."

When her momma, in tears, read those words out loud to her over the phone, Gillian cried with her.

"I think it's time to move on," Louise said. So they arranged for him to come to Gold Creek Gap for the reception.

Will had promised Gillian and her momma a beautiful reception, and by gosh, he was giving them one. Well, the women had done the actual planning, but he was the one who set the date six months after the wedding. At first they'd planned to hold it at the church, but then they decided to wait until the house was built, so they could hold it there, hence the delay.

Louise had argued about the house at first, saying there was nothing wrong with her trailer. After all, she had a beautiful garden. Will and Gillian had assured her that while nothing was wrong with her mobile home, they would like it if she'd stay in the sprawling new home they had built by the lake and take care of it when they weren't around. Since they only made it there a couple of weekends a month at best, due to Gillian's tour dates, Louise had the run of the house. This had given her the freedom and time to plan the reception, and since Gillian was too busy living her life as a music artist to help like she wanted to, Aunt Cher was happy to pitch in. Gillian's only request was that there be sushi. Her mom and Cher thought that was crazy, but she said she'd promised Will.

The day had finally arrived, and Gillian and Will were thrilled with the lights draping along the deck overlooking the lake. There were people dancing, children splashing down on the bank, and more food and wine than anyone could ever consume.

Louise stood there with a smile on her face, satisfied at how the rich and famous mingled with the small town folks from Gold Creek Gap and from Will's hometown only a few hours away. *This is how life is supposed to be*, she thought. People being together, not caring about where they came from or how much money they had.

Her daughter waved, and Louise made her way over to the happy couple. Never had Gillian looked so beautiful or so happy standing with her husband and all her friends. She especially loved that Tasha. She'd been a big help with the reception. Louise thought it was sweet of Gillian and Will to let her have this reception, since she'd missed their wedding, but they didn't realize she was even happier that her daughter had found a man who treated her so well and who made her so happy.

"Thank you for all this, Momma." Gillian kissed her mother. "You're the best. And you too, Aunt Cher."

Aunt Cher hurried over. "Anything for you, sweetheart, and you too, Will."

"We sure are thankful," he told her with a grin, but then his smile faltered. Gillian, Louise and Cher turned in the direction Will was looking. A reunion was about to happen, and he hoped his wife's heart wouldn't be broken in the process.

Gillian stared at Cooper Heart as he made his way through the crowd. He was handsomely dressed in a western cut suit, and his eyes were glued to Gillian. Louise turned to see her daughter's face. She and Will reached for her at the same time.

"If you've changed your mind, it's OK," Will said. "I'll make him leave right now."

"I want him to stay," Gillian said, steeling herself as he approached. It seemed like a long time, but when he finally reached her, all the anger that'd gathered in her heart evaporated. She wasn't the same little girl who'd stood out on the front porch daily waiting for him to come home.

They stared at each other, Gillian's heart nearly flying out of her chest.

"Did you mean what you said in that article?" she asked.

He nodded, his eyes glistening.

"Please forgive me, Gilly," he said, and the sound of his voice calling her by her nickname broke her in two.

"Daddy." She threw herself into his arms, not caring what he'd done wrong. They'd have to sort through all of that later, but for now, he was home, and it was all she cared about.

"Holy praises," Aunt Cher muttered. Louise hadn't said anything, which led Gillian to believe that her dad and mom had talked before the reception. She vaguely tried to imagine what that would have been like for her momma, but she didn't look angry. Life is short, is what her momma always said. There's no time to waste. Gillian smiled as she breathed in her dad's scent. He still wore the same cologne. It brought back a flood of happy memories of the times they'd spent together, before he'd left.

When they finally let go of each other, Cooper looked at Will. He offered his hand.

"Will."

"Cooper. How you been?"

Cooper smiled weakly. "I never saw this one coming, son, but I couldn't be happier to know Gillian's with you." Will nodded.

Finally, Cooper turned to his sister, Cher. She leaned forward and gave him a kiss, because she was like that, forgiving, and so loyal to everyone she loved that it drove everyone else crazy.

With obvious affection and regret reflected in the lines of his face, he turned toward Louise. He simply stood with his hat in his hands, staring at her like a lost puppy. Louise cast a look at Gillian and sighed. She'd always had a soft spot for lost puppies, dang it.

"Come here," Louise said, and drew him to her. He wrapped his arms around her, and while everyone knew he had as much to work out later with Louise as with Gillian, they all nodded their approval and passed out tissues.

Will left Gillian for a minute to speak to the band, who'd stopped when they realized something was happening. They started playing again, and Cooper escorted Louise onto the dance floor. Everyone smiled as the band crooned Elvis' *Love Me Tender* and went back to dancing.

Will held his hand out to Gillian. "What do ya say, little darlin'?"

She smiled at his reference to their Elvis wedding. "I say, we still gotta lotta livin' to do."

He pulled her close, and they danced through the evening, until they stole away when nobody was looking. They drove to the back of a field by the river and spent the rest of the night under the sycamore trees in the bed of the pickup truck underneath the stars.

# Also Available from Tina Ann Forkner

# A Note from Tina Ann Forkner

Dear Reader,

I've always wanted to write about Nashville. Everything about it fascinates me, from the city life to the Southern food, but I love the music the most. My interest in the music industry started as a kid when I watched my sister sing all over Oklahoma and Arkansas. She was amazing. I could never hold a tune very well so I contented myself with listening to her sing while I wrote stories. We used to dream of her moving to Nashville and me becoming a journalist. With a few plot twists, we both achieved our dreams. She had a decade-long career behind the scenes in Nashville, and I became a published novelist.

Cheri and I have always encouraged each other to follow our dreams. Now, all these years later, I'm writing a book about Nashville.

I hope you enjoyed reading *Nashville by Heart* as much as I enjoyed writing it. And if you did, I would love for you to tell others. Thanks for reading!

All the best,
*Tina Ann Forkner*

P.S. You can stay up to date on my new releases and special sales by subscribing to my newsletter. You can sign up here: bit.ly/BookNewsFromTina.

# Acknowledgments

Thank you, dear readers, for loving the romantic aspects of my women's fiction enough that I was inspired to write you a romance novel. Thank you to Ann Garvin and the Tall Poppy Writers. I am so honored to be part of such a talented group of women authors. Many thanks to Author Amy Sue Nathan for bringing out the best in my story, and to fellow Wyoming author Joanne Kennedy for thinking the book was good enough to provide a lovely endorsement. Thanks to my coffee writers group in Cheyenne for encouraging me to bring this book to readers. I don't make it to all the coffees, but I appreciate all of you.

A special thanks to the Wyoming book community. You have always been beyond supportive and welcoming of my work. It means a lot to this Oklahoma girl who after two decades of living here is proud to be from Wyoming.

Much love to my daughter, Hannah, who is an incredible person and shares my love of books. Thank you to my mother-in-law Nancy for raising the hero I would one day marry. And special thanks to my mom, Barbara, who when asked what she'd think if her daughter wrote a romance novel responded with, "Why not? Romance makes the world go round." After more than fifty years with my sweet dad, my lovely mom would know.

Most of all, thank you to my beautiful sister, Cheri Kaufman, for giving me a behind-the-scenes look inside Nashville during your marvelous decade working in the music industry. You always knew it would end up in a book, right?

# About the Author

**Tina Ann Forkner** is a freelance editor and writer, a speaker, and the author of *Ruby Among Us*, *Rose House*, *The Real Thing*, and *Waking Up Joy* (a Virginia Romance Writers 2015 HOLT Medallion Finalist). She lives in Cheyenne, Wyoming with her husband where she teaches writing workshops to children and adults. She is also a substitute teacher for her local school district and a volunteer for the Laramie County Library Foundation. Learn more at TinaAnnForkner.com, and sign up to receive her newsletter at bit.ly/BookNewsFromTina.

Made in the USA
Columbia, SC
28 December 2020